EXECUTION DAY

The Holy Warriors escorted Blade out of his cell, through the corridors, and up the stairs to the surface. After days of darkness the sunlight dazzled his eyes, and they had to adjust before he could see the thousands of silent, waiting people surrounding the temple in the hot still air. Blade watched each victim seized and dragged to the great white stone block, where a priest carved open their stomachs and groins in the form of bats' wings. Blade was next in line, and he would have to make his move soon.

Now! He lunged into a group of warriors, snatching their axes from their belts. Ribs caved in, blood spurted from throats, and bones cracked as Blade carved his way through the hysterical mass of seething bodies. He chopped and slashed and parried, his strikes clanging off sword blades or chopping deep into flesh and bone, clearing a path for his escape.

But the Holy Warriors were emerging from the ebbing and floundering crowd, and blood began to trickle from small wounds in Blade's body. His remaining axe, which suddenly seemed to weigh a hundred pounds, was losing its edge. Blade realized that he wasn't going to get out of this one . . .

The Richard Blade Series

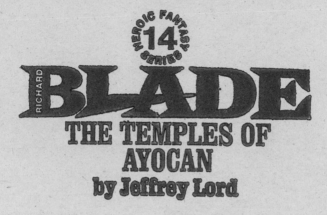

HEROIC FANTASY SERIES 14

RICHARD BLADE

THE TEMPLES OF AYOCAN

by Jeffrey Lord

PINNACLE BOOKS • NEW YORK CITY

BLADE: THE TEMPLES OF AYOCAN

Copyright © 1975 by Lyle Kenyon Engel

An original Pinnacle Books edition, published for the first time anywhere.

ISBN: 0-523-00623-3

First printing, May 1975
Second printing, July 1975
Third printing, April 1976

Printed in the United States of America

PINNACLE BOOKS, INC.
275 Madison Avenue
New York, N.Y. 10016

THE TEMPLES OF AYOCAN

CHAPTER 1

Making a living by being whisked off to other dimensions on short notice has advantages. Also disadvantages. At the moment, Richard Blade was more conscious of the disadvantages.

The voice on the telephone was that of a young woman in a mighty rage. Even so it was a beautiful voice, as beautiful as the body it was coming from. Blade had learned to know the body intimately over several nights during the past few weeks. But then the message had come from J— get ready for another trip into Dimension X. So he had called Cynthia to tell her that he would be out of town for the next few weeks or months.

"No, I can't give you an address where you can reach me. I'll be traveling around too much for that."

"You're trying to give me the brush-off, Dick. I wish you'd come right out and say, 'Get lost, Cynthia.' I'd have more respect for you if you did. You men are all alike. Stallions in bed, but when it comes to something like this, you haven't got the courage of a cockroach!"

"Now, damn it all, Cynthia, I'm not saying get lost because I don't want—"

"*You* don't want? What about *me* not wanting something? We were so good together, Dick. I can't stand it for you to just walk off like this. Especially when you won't tell me where you're going, or anything! You just want to go off tomcatting around, and don't want to tell me!"

"Cynthia, you're being ridicu— Hello, Cynthia? Cynthia?"

The line was dead.

Blade put the receiver back in the cradle. Then he let out his frustration and annoyance in language much stronger than merely "Damn it all!"

There definitely were disadvantages to being the key man in Project Dimension X. When the demands of the Project came down on even his most casual relationships like DDT on a mosquito and killed them just as dead, it got more than a little annoying. Oh, well, Cynthia had been showing signs of getting possessive, perhaps even marriage-minded. That would have meant telling her goodbye sooner or later, but certainly not now. Lord Leighton had barged in properly!

At least Blade knew that he would not have too much trouble finding another congenial woman after he returned from Dimension X, even if Cynthia had given him the brush-off. For Blade, this was simply recognizing a fact. He was inevitably attractive to women. And why not? Six feet plus, two hundred and ten pounds of athletic Englishman, pushing forty but looking ten years younger, radiating charm, vitality, and virility. Not a fluent talker, but not tongue-tied either. And with the indefinable but definite glamor that hangs around a man who always seems to be on the move, whose scars suggest an active and even dangerous life, but who never talks about what he does. To almost all who knew him, Blade's profession was a mystery.

He hoped it would stay that way, considering what it really was. Tomorrow morning Blade would go to the Tower of London. A secret elevator would carry him two hundred feet down to an equally secret underground complex that housed the most advanced computers in the world. These computers were the brainchildren of Lord Leighton, England's most brilliant and most irascible scientist. Blade's brain would be directly linked to these computers.

2

And then he would be hurled, as naked as the day he was born, into another dimension, where anything and everything might happen. Animals that walked like men, savage warriors, decadent super-civilizations, even non-human intelligences from outer space—he had met them all. And so far he had survived each meeting. Thirteen times, to be exact.

Not only natural gifts, but training and experience had kept him alive. He had been one of the top agents for the secret intelligence agency MI6 for the better part of twenty years. He had learned to be a professional survivor long before Lord Leighton had even dreamed of the computer that made the Dimension X Project possible.

He hoped that sooner rather than later Lord Leighton and J would come up with someone equally qualified. He was tough, he was smart, so far he had been lucky, and by temperament he was an adventurer in a century where adventurers too often found themselves the odd man out. But he could push his luck only so far. If it ran out before Lord Leighton and J found anybody else, Project Dimension X would be left high and dry. The whole purpose of the Project was to explore and perhaps someday exploit Dimension X for knowledge and raw materials that England could use. Without somebody able to travel into Dimension X, this would become impossible.

So Lord Leighton was looking for somebody new. J, head of MI6 and Blade's guide and mentor for twenty years, was looking for somebody new. And the prime minister, who had backed Project Dimension X and all its host of subprojects to the tune of many millions of pounds, was looking for somebody new. But so far Blade was in no danger of joining the ranks of the unemployed.

He went over to the sideboard and pulled out a bottle of whiskey. Four fingers of Scotch, a dash of soda, and he had a good stiff nightcap. He raised the glass in a silent toast to his unknown successor, whoever he might be, and drained it. Then he went to bed.

He was up early the next morning, and had a large

breakfast. He had no idea how long he would be in Dimension X before he could find food. The last time he had gone across, Lord Leighton had sent along a comprehensive survival kit with several days' survival rations. But Blade had arrived with nothing and as naked as he had all the previous times. For safety's sake he preferred to assume the same thing would happen this time. Blade's experience as a field agent and then as an explorer of Dimension X had taught him the wisdom of assuming the worst.

A taxi took him to the Tower of London through a chill, gray, unremarkable winter day. And the expressions of the Special Branch men guarding the entrance to the complex were as chill as the weather. Was that look something they were trained to assume, or did it come naturally after one had been a Special Branch operative long enough?

In the complex itself, two hundred feet below, the gloomy weather and the gloomy Special Branch men seemed like a bad dream. Light gleamed off polished floors and walls, and the air was warm. All the guarding was done by invisible electronic sentinels, some of them Lord Leighton's own inventions, others from the Ministry of Defense's bag of tricks. And J was waiting for Blade when the elevator door slid open, to walk with him down the corridor to the computers.

Blade looked more closely than usual at J as they walked side by side. If J was aging at all, he was doing so as imperturbably as he did everything else. Perhaps he had acquired a few more wrinkles in the years since Project Dimension X had begun. Certainly some of his still thick gray hair had definitely begun to turn white. But J still looked more like an aging senior bureaucrat in the Ministry of Agriculture or something equally prosaic than what he was—one of the most experienced and respected spymasters in the world, with a career of achievement going all the way back to World War I.

Certainly nothing showed in J's voice as he chatted with Blade. "Lord Leighton says we're going to be reverting to the old procedure this time."

4

"No survival kit?"

"Quite right. He thinks your—'materializing'—in Dimension X well above ground level the last time wasn't an accident. He thinks the extra mass of the survival kit wasn't quite compensated for by the adjustments to the computer, so you went through in an unbalanced state. Physically, that is."

Blade nodded. "And he's worried that the next time I might pop through into Dimension X a hundred feet up, instead of just thirty?"

"Quite so. And go smash when you come down. Lord Leighton doesn't want that, not at all."

"How nice of him," said Blade. But there was a grin on his face that took some of the sarcastic bite out of his words. Lord Leighton was determined to appear the unwavering and completely emotionless scientist, with no concern for anything but the results of his experiments. Perhaps he had really once been that unconcerned about Blade's welfare. But no longer. Both Blade and J knew that Lord Leighton had come as close to affection and concern for Blade as he could. In fact, he was probably almost as concerned about Blade's welfare as he was about his computers. Not as concerned as J, though, for J loved Blade like a son.

"Very," said J, matching Blade's tone and expression. "He's going to try some experiments to get the computer adjusted properly for the survival kit. But they'll take quite a while, along with everything else he has to do. So for the time being you'll be going into Dimension X—ah— in the altogether again." Blade nodded.

They passed through another door, and the scrutiny of its electronic watchdogs, and then they were in the computer rooms themselves. Blade nodded and smiled to the white-coated technicians manning consoles and working on breadboard layouts. By now all of them knew him by sight, and he knew most of them. The turnover among the staff of the underground complex was slow. Once Lord

5

Leighton got hold of a qualified man, he was reluctant to let him go.

Finally the last and smallest door slid noiselessly shut behind them. They were in Lord Leighton's inner sanctum.

It was also the place where Lord Leighton seemed most at home. Almost anywhere in the outside world, he was an unimpressive, even grotesque figure—hunchbacked, white-haired, scuttling about on polio-twisted legs, his wrinkled and mottled face showing his eighty-plus years with brutal clarity. He looked like an aging and unfriendly gnome, with only the bright dark eyes showing any signs of health and vigor. But among the computers he had created, he looked different—very normal, very much in command.

There was a brief exchange of greetings and pleasantries as Blade and J entered. But Lord Leighton was obviously impatient to get things moving. From the pattern of lights on the master console of the central computer, Blade realized that the main sequence was already underway. Within a few minutes the computer would be ready to hurl him into Dimension X.

With no survival kit to worry about, his own preparations were no different from what he had gone through a dozen times before. In fact, the preparations had become a drill, like field-stripping a machine gun or making a parachute jump. He had learned both during his commando training. But it was easier to be careful with the gun or the parachute. With them, how much care one took could make a big difference, even the difference between life and death. With the trips into Dimension X, nothing in the preparations seemed to make any difference. He always arrived naked as a baby, his head throbbing.

But why take chances? With as much care as ever, he stripped off his own clothing. Then he smeared every inch of his skin with the foul-smelling black gunk that was supposed to prevent electrical burns. Perhaps it actually did. Then he knotted a loincloth around his middle, no doubt as futilely as all the times before.

He stepped out and walked to the chair in the center

6

of the room. The seat was cold against his bare thighs as he sat down. His head almost brushed the glass roof of the cubicle that held the chair, while his feet rested on the rubber mat where it stood. Around him the huge consoles of the main computer rose to the rock ceiling of the chamber. In their gray-crackled finish the consoles seemed almost as ancient and solid as the rock of the walls and roof.

J stepped back and sat down in the observer's chair, while Lord Leighton went busily to work. If there was anything slow or aged about his hands, one would never know it to watch him putting the electrodes on Blade. There were scores of them, in the shape of gleaming metal cobra's heads, leading into scores of wires in a dozen different colors, the wires linking Blade to the computer.

Now Blade was fully wired in place, with electrodes hanging from every part of his body that they could grip. Lord Leighton finished his visual inspection of all the readouts. He never omitted this, no matter how many automatic controls and monitoring devices he installed in the computers. "The human mind is still the best monitoring device when you can't be sure in advance of what you're going to find," he often said. Then he turned to Blade, ran one hand through his scanty white hair, and poised the other over the red master switch.

"Are you comfortable, Richard?"

Blade would have shrugged if the straps and electrodes on him had permitted. "I'd have to say I'm as comfortable as I could expect, under the circumstances." Not that his discomfort or comfort would make any difference in another few seconds, when he was whirled off to Dimension X. But Lord Leighton obviously wanted to hear that his guinea pig was comfortable. So why not humor the man?

Lord Leighton smiled thinly. Blade fixed his gaze on the gnarled hand as it drifted down to close over the switch. He kept it fixed as the switch slowly moved down in its slot, toward the red line—and over it.

Sudden, terrible, total disorientation struck Blade, all

7

his senses blacking out at once. There was an instant when he was not even aware of his own body, and barely aware of the workings of his own mind. There was just enough self-awareness left for him to feel a stabbing, numbing fear.

He was dying.

The computer had finally run amuck and destroyed his mind.

This was the last moment of awareness he would have, before he went out forever like a snuffed candle.

If he had had a throat, he would have screamed in that moment. But he had to scream inside his mind. And then the moment passed.

Light and sound and the sensation of movement returned to him in an explosive rush. For a moment he wanted to scream again, as the sensations poured down on him like a waterfall, making his mind reel. Then his mind reacted and stabilized itself, sorting out all the impressions tearing at it into something coherent.

He was sliding down an immense shimmering black slope, whirling around and around as he did so. Overhead pulsed a glaring sky filled with terrible silver light, so brilliant that he had to narrow his eyes to keep from being dazzled. There was no feeling of air rushing past him as he plunged downward, no feeling of friction with the blackness under him. It was as though the black surface was so perfectly lubricated that he slipped over it as effortlessly as a bit of dandelion fluff.

Then the air around him began to grow thicker, seemingly trying to wrap itself around him and slow his passage. He began to feel as if he was falling ever more slowly into a bottomless mass of thin, watery dough—sticky, clammy, and cold. He found himself holding his breath, then discovered that the dough was growing thicker and beginning to tighten around his chest. Each time he breathed out, he found it harder to breathe in again. Then he could not breathe in at all, and once again he felt a moment of panic. And then there was blackness.

8

CHAPTER 2

Being able to breathe again told Blade that he had made the shift into the new dimension. For a time he did not try to move, except for the muscles in his chest. He lay where he had landed, savoring the luxury of cool air flowing in and out of his body. He did not even bother to open his eyes.

When he did, bright sunlight stabbed into them, which did not make his throbbing head feel any better. He closed his eyes again and turned his head to one side and kept it in that position until the headache had faded. Then he opened his eyes, lifted his head, and looked around him.

He first saw mountains—high mountains, snowcapped, rearing jaggedly against a blue sky. For a moment the mountains seemed so close that he thought he could reach out and touch them—or they could rise up and topple over on him.

Then his vision cleared, and perspective returned. It was the crystal clear air and the flat land between him and the mountains that made them look so close. In fact they must be forty or fifty or even more miles away. It was hard to tell how high their summits rose into the flawless blue sky, but some of them must be close to twenty-five thousand feet. From one jagged peak a long white plume of snow whipped out in the wind, like a feather in a lady's hat.

Slowly, flexing each limb to see if it still worked, Blade rose to his feet. He was as naked as ever, but apparently

9

uninjured. He went through a quick series of exercises to make absolutely sure, and to work some of the tension out of his mind. Physical activity had always helped him relieve mental strain.

Even a short spurt of physical exercise made his breath come short, quick, and hard. This was something he hadn't anticipated while he lay resting. Even the place where he stood must be at a fairly high altitude, ten or twelve thousand feet above sea level at least. Air this thin would not hold heat very well.

For the moment it seemed to be near noon, for the sun blazed hotly almost straight down from the clear sky. But it would be cold at night—colder than Blade wanted to face naked and unequipped.

Now he made a more careful survey of his surroundings. All around him was a level blue-gray plain—hard, dusty earth with patches of gravel and boulders. There was not a tree in sight, and precious little vegetation of any sort.

Far to the south a glimmer of darker blue broke the monotony of the plain. Blade narrowed his eyes against the glare of the sun from the miles of bare rock and examined the south still more carefully. The blueness might be just a miles-wide outcropping of another kind of rock, darker that that of the plain. But the way it gleamed? Everything in Blade's survival training and field experience shouted (or whispered) "Water!" Certainly there was nothing else within sight that looked as much like water. Even more certainly, there was nothing here offering a better chance of survival than a large body of fresh water. Probably there would be fish and vegetation, perhaps human settlements along its shores. Certainly any human settlements he was likely to find within easy walking distance would be along the lake.

Unless the water was brackish? He swore mentally at his ingrained habit of considering all the possibilities, even the worst ones. Then he firmly pushed the thought down. Where else in all this endless plain did he have *any* chance

10

of finding what he needed to survive? When his conditioned pessimism was finally silent, he headed south.

He moved along briskly, trying not to exert himself enough to work up a sweat. There was no point in wasting any moisture if he could avoid it. Distances were deceptive on this high plain, as he already knew. That glimmer of water might have come from twenty miles away.

He loped onward, his shadow black against the lighter blue-gray of the earth at his feet. Sun and wind had powdered a thin layer of that earth, and as he moved along he left footprints and kicked up dust. Under that thin layer the earth was nearly as solid as the rocks that lay in large patches everywhere.

It was a drab land. The only color nearer than the mountains was occasional patches of white gravel and even rarer patches of scrubby black-green bushes and vines. These were mostly huddled in the lee of the larger rocks. Not surprising, in this land where a wind from those mountains could sweep fifty miles unchecked, stripping the land bare, grinding down even boulders with clouds of wind-driven dust. This was a land that had been here long before men—if indeed there were any in this dimension. And it would be here long after they had gone, if they ever came, and it would show no signs of either their coming or their going.

The blue on the horizon spread wider and wider as Blade moved south, and the sun began to creep down from overhead, toward the mountains. By the time it was halfway down in the sky, Blade knew that the blueness must indeed be water. By the time the sun hovered just above the highest peaks, Blade was within a mile of the shore of the lake. And by the time darkness was falling, he was standing by the water's edge.

Seen close up, the water was an incredibly rich blue. It was impossible for Blade to judge how far it stretched— neither to the south nor to the east could he see any shore. At this altitude it had to be a lake, but a lake the size of

11

an inland sea. And it was fresh water. One taste reassured Blade on that point. Whatever he might die from in this new dimension, it would not be thirst.

For many hundreds of yards back from the water's edge, the shore of the lake was heavily overgrown with low-slung black-green bushes. These bore large yellow flowers that looked somewhat like sunflowers except that the mass of seeds in the middle of the blossom was bright red instead of brownish. Blade wondered if the red seeds were as edible as sunflower seeds. If they were, he was in no danger of starving either.

But he was in danger of getting very cold very quickly. The thin air of the high plain was rapidly losing its heat now that the sun was gone. A chill breeze crept down from the distant mountains, blowing across his bare skin and bit by bit robbing his body of its heat. He bent down and took hold of one of the bushes, trying to break it off or pull it up out of the ground. A layer of leafy branches under him and another over him might not make the most comfortable bed for a good night's sleep, but they would at least be something between his bare skin and the cold.

The bushes were tough and their bark scraped at his fingers, which were red and sore by the time he had broken off half a dozen branches. The broken ends dripped a sticky lemon-yellow sap. Blade bent down and sniffed at it. A strong vegetable smell, but underneath it something else, tantalizingly faint, so faint he couldn't define or describe it. But definitely appealing. He sniffed at the sap more vigorously, then suddenly pulled himself to a stop and threw the branch down on the ground.

That faint, underlying element in the smell of the sap was something—Blade didn't know what—insidiously attractive. He had been within seconds of smearing the sap over his nostrils, to absorb more and still more of the odor. And then what? What would a massive dose of whatever lurked in the sap have done to him? He didn't know and he didn't want to find out, at least not here and now. All he needed now was an overdose of narcotics while he was fighting to survive and keep warm on the lonely shores of this lake. He continued breaking off branches, but he was very careful now to keep them away from his face. He even tried to keep the sap from getting on his skin. He had no way of knowing whether or not it could be absorbed into his body through the skin.

By the time Blade had piled on the ground what he hoped would be enough branches, it was almost completely dark. Only the faintest orange glimmer beyond the mountains gave him any sense of direction. The lake stretched out endlessly away into the darkness, featureless and now black instead of blue. The wind had died, and even the faint splashing of little waves on the gravel of the beach had died away with it. For the moment, this was a dimension of total loneliness, almost total darkness, and silence except for the sound of his own breathing and footsteps.

Blade was getting ready to burrow down into his bed of branches when he suddenly realized that there was no longer total darkness out on the lake. Lights had suddenly appeared, faint, distant, and wavering, but unmistakable. Blade counted nine of them, stretched out in a long line across the lake. They shone a pale yellow-orange, and slowly but steadily they were coming closer. Their approach was too steady, too purposeful, for anything natural.

The line spread out wider and wider, until it seemed to stretch halfway across the lake horizon. Blade realized that if the line kept on all the way to the shore, he would end up almost in the middle of it. Slowly and cautiously, he rose to a crouching position, and moved away from his piled branches. He would have liked to scatter them so that they gave no sign of his presence, but there was no time for that. The lights were coming on faster now. Blade could hear a distant but fast-swelling chant as they did so.

He slipped up the slope from the beach, taking care to

avoid softer patches of ground where he might leave footprints. Fifty yards up the slope, he came to a particularly thick patch of the bushes, some of them eight feet high. The close-grown rough branches were hard to push apart and painful to slip through. But when he had done so, he could crouch almost invisible to anyone on the beach.

The chant coming out of the darkness was definitely getting louder now. With relief Blade recognized human voices—at least forty or fifty of them, all chanting together to a beat set by two deep-toned drums. He had encountered a fair number of nonhuman or semihuman beings in his Dimension X travels, but he always preferred to at least start by dealing with human beings. Not that human beings were necessarily that much more predictable than nonhumans, or less likely to shoot first and ask questions afterward. It was more a question of what contributed most to his own peace of mind.

The lights kept growing brighter, the chant kept growing louder. Now Blade could make out words, and understand them. Once again Lord Leighton's computer had done its incomprehensible work on his brain, altering it so that he understood and responded in the language of the new dimension, however strange it might be.

The chant was a repetition of a single set of sentences, in a complex and varying pattern. Blade could pick out at least three different parts, and every fourth repetition they seemed to shift key entirely.

Over and over again the words came:

"Hail, flower of life! Hail, flower of death! We come to you in the service of Ayocan. We come to you in the judgment of Ayocan."

Ayocan? thought Blade. King, priest, saint, devil, god, spirit? And the flower of life/death? Blade had a sudden chilling thought. Could the "flower" be the one growing on the bushes where he was lurking, the bushes with the narcotic sap? There didn't seem to be anything else living here that might match the description. And what were the

14

people approaching across the lake planning to do with the bushes?

He had no time to answer these questions, or ask himself any more. Suddenly even more yellow-orange light was shining from the lake. Narrowing his eyes against the new glare, Blade saw that behind each of the nine original lights a second one was now burning, brighter than the first. Then the original lights all went out, suddenly, simultaneously, with almost military precision. Now Blade could see what was approaching him across the lake—and who.

CHAPTER 3

Nine long outrigger canoes were approaching Blade across the lake, each sixty-odd feet long and filled with men. He counted more than thirty men in each canoe. All were thin-faced and brown-skinned, but otherwise they seemed divided into two groups.

One group was obviously warriors. They carried long swords that gleamed in the torchlight with the sheen of polished bronze, and daggers and short-handled axes that seemed to be made of polished green stone. They wore dark blue armor from neck to wrists and ankles, consisting of dyed leather patches sewn on a cloth backing, and on their heads they wore vividly dyed orange, red, yellow, and green helmets plumed with white feathers. About twenty of the men in each boat were warriors. Two stood at the bow, tending the torch that poured out yellow-orange light, one stood at the stern, tending the steering oar, and the others paddled.

The other men in each canoe were—what? They wore only simple flowing yellow-orange robes, with a bit of blue embroidery at the neck, and no weapons that Blade could see. Their heads were not only shaved bald but apparently oiled, from the way they glistened in the light. Their faces were also oiled, and cheeks, forehead, and neck were marked with cryptic signs in white. Each of them, Blade noticed, carried a large blue cloth bag also marked with white signs and slung from a blue leather belt at his waist. It was these men who were keeping up the chant about the flower of life and death.

16

That was all Blade was able to make out before the warriors suddenly drew in their paddles. The canoes floated in to shore and grounded on the gravel beach with gentle scraping sounds. The warriors in the bows of each one leaped down into the water, carrying a large stone with a rope tied around it, and dropped this improvised anchor on the beach. In each canoe a yellow-robe rose to his feet and went forward to the torch in the bow, pouring some liquid over it from a small bronze ewer he took from the bottom of the boat. Each torch blazed up still more brightly, spreading yellow-orange light still farther up the slope from the beach.

In Blade's mind the need to be cautious fought a brief battle with the need to make contact with the human population of this dimension. Normally he would not have hesitated to step out from his hiding place and greet the men in the canoes. But the shaven-headed men looked too much like priests—priests of Ayocan, perhaps? And where there were priests, there was often some religious rite that it was ill-advised for a stranger to interrupt. The best plan for the moment was to stay under cover, watch, and wait. The torches were so bright now that making a run for it undetected would probably be impossible. Particularly with two hundred or more warriors ready to pursue him. Blade lowered himself into a more comfortable position and settled down to follow his own advice.

As soon as the canoes were safely beached and anchored, the warriors put away their paddles and began climbing out. They splashed onto the beach and formed a double line extending inland from the bow of each canoe. Then it was the priests' turn. Without breaking their chant, they filed out of the canoes and onto the shore, unfastening their bags as they went and holding them up high over their heads. When all had reached dry ground, the leader of each file barked a single word.

"Nolk!"

And all the priests went down on their knees, placing their bags reverently on the ground in front of them, each

17

at the base of one of the bushes. Except for the breathing of many men, silence fell over the shore.

Definitely a religious rite, thought Blade. He was sorry he had not made a run for it when he first saw the yellow-orange lights. Now it was even more dangerous than before to try to escape. Since the priests did not seem to be coming far up the slope, the remains of his bough-bed might pass unnoticed, he hoped.

Now each priest picked up his bag, opened it, and pulled out a large curved knife, like a pruning knife, and a small brass bottle. With a quick slash of the knife each priest cut through the bush in front of him. Then he picked it up, and dipped the broken end into the bottle. Finally, he laid the bush gently and carefully aside. Blade noticed that the cutoff end now gleamed black.

The priests then rose to their feet, the chant sounded again, and each took two steps forward. Then they knelt again and repeated the ritual. Slash—dip—lay aside. And again, and again. Blade realized with a chilling shock that they were moving rapidly up the slope toward him, toward where he had mutilated more than a dozen of the bushes.

The intervals between the cutting of bushes were growing longer now, and the priests were also fanning out as they climbed. They formed a solid line nearly a quarter of a mile from end to end, with Blade still near the center. Behind them as they advanced came the warriors, picking up the bushes as gently as they would have picked up newborn babies and carrying them back to the canoes. Unless both priests and warriors were blind, they must see those broken branches soon.

Blade did not have much longer to wait. Suddenly two priests broke off their chant. Their voices rose in howls of outrage that brought all the chanting to a sudden halt. Priests and warriors alike scurried toward the noisy two, gathered around them, and raised their own voices in lamentations. Blade saw that the two priests in the middle were each holding up a broken-off branch with one hand, and

18

gesturing violently with the other. In the babble of voices rising into the night Blade could not make out a single coherent word. But he could certainly recognize tones of anger, outrage, and grim determination.

Obviously he had committed some sort of sacrilege by taking the branches. And there went practically any hope of quickly getting on good terms with these people. It was tempting to throw caution to the winds and try making a run for it. But Blade's trained judgment of the situation told him he would not get far. The warriors would be up with him before he got clear of the bushes. And he had no desire to run like a rabbit and end up being hunted down like one.

Besides, his best remaining chance was to stay and try to make the best fight possible. Barbarian warriors could understand and appreciate courage in battle better than anything else. He might be able to get the warriors to take him prisoner by a show of courage and skill. There were the priests, of course, but priests were always unpredictable. Certainly he had nothing to lose.

With only small cracklings of branches, Blade crawled out of his hiding place. The warriors striding up the slope did not see him as he crouched in the shadows of the clump of bushes. Then he stood up, and they did see him. The two who saw him first raised shouts of triumph and rage, making the rest of the searchers spin around and stare at Blade. The gathering around the two priests broke up in a gabble of voices. Blade saw drawn swords gleaming in the torchlight, and the heads of axes glistening. He made no move to run or hide, but stood calmly in the open, hands at his sides.

The first two warriors moved toward him, taking care to avoid damaging the bushes. Blade shifted a few steps to the left and dropped into an unarmed-combat fighting stance, balanced on the balls of his feet, fists raised. Both warriors were coming at him with their swords in the right hand and their axes in the left. Blade kept a particularly close watch on the axes. If they were throwing axes, he might need more luck than he liked to imagine to make a good showing in this fight. He wanted the warriors at close quarters, where his unarmed-combat skills would give him an advantage.

The warriors spread apart as they approached, until they were coming in almost on either side of Blade. He drifted back a few steps, so he could keep both in sight. They spread still farther apart, again trying to get around his flanks. But now they were so far apart that they could not support each other. Blade saw that, and also saw that the next step the right-hand one took would bring him into the open, with nothing between him and Blade.

The warrior took that step. Blade sprang forward, fists lunging. He came down within striking distance of the warrior. His right fist flashed past the man's rising sword and smashed into his jaw. The warrior's head snapped back, his eyes rolled up in his head, and he collapsed backward, spitting blood and teeth. As he went down Blade broke his sword-arm with a left-handed karate chop and snatched the sword out of the air. He had just time to raise it before the second warrior charged in, sword guarding and axe raised to strike overhand. By sheer speed and strength Blade smashed the man's guard down and split his skull open like a melon. The axe dropped from his wavering hand, and that too Blade plucked out of the air.

Blade turned toward the other warriors and brandished both sword and axe high in the air. They caught the torchlight and threw off sparks of yellow-orange. He shouted at the warriors, "Come on, little men! If you are men, that is. Two hundred of you, only one of me. Isn't that even odds, at least? Or does it take three hundred of you to meet one *real* warrior?"

His insults got the reaction he was hoping for. Angry growls and muttered curses rose from among the warriors. Blade shifted again, still farther up the slope, and watched two more warriors move toward him.

This time Blade attacked first. He could move faster through the bushes, for he did not have to worry about damaging them. Vaulting high over one of the lower bushes, he landed squarely between the two warriors. Before they recovered from the surprise, he had whirled to the left, slashing low with his sword. The warrior brought his sword down to guard while raising his axe to strike. This opened his left side and armpit to Blade, who struck hard with his own axe. He felt bone crunch under the axe, and the warrior choked, coughed blood, and fell gasping and writhing to the ground. Blade leaped high, smashing both feet down on his back as he lay, and the warrior abruptly stopped writhing.

Now Blade leaped from his victim's body to face the man's partner. This warrior was either more skilled or more cautious. He stood on the defensive, guarding with both axe and sword, his black eyes never leaving Blade's face. Blade feinted several times with both sword and axe, but the warrior's responses were fast and sure, and left no openings. Blade realized this was a more dangerous opponent than the first three. But he couldn't afford to let the fight go on much longer. Every extra minute would give the other warriors more confidence, and perhaps a chance for a sneak blow from the rear.

Blade hefted the short-handled axe, assessing the balance. Perhaps it wasn't used for throwing, but that didn't mean it couldn't be. The balance seemed right. He took two steps back, to give himself room then his arm rose and swung back. The warrior rushed forward, Blade's arm also snapped forward, and the axe flashed through the air and squarely into the warrior's chest. Its weight and the razor-sharp edge buried it deep. Blood oozed from around it. The warrior stood for a moment as if turned to stone, his eyes staring blankly down at the thing in his chest. Then his knees gave and he plunged forward on his face. Blade stepped forward, picked up the fallen man's axe, and again faced his enemies.

Some of the warriors were still cursing angrily, but others were muttering uncertainly. Blade's quick disposal of four of them had certainly made an impression. Even

21

the ones who were shaking their fists at him did so from a safe distance, and he did not notice any of them moving in to the attack.

Then the chief priest joined the warriors. There was nothing to distinguish him from the other priests except his manner—but when he gave orders, they were obeyed. Blade could not make out what the man was saying, but he could once again recognize the tone. Crisp and angry, but well controlled, the priest was telling the warriors not to be such children as to let one man frighten them off. As the priest went on, Blade saw some of the warriors begin to edge in toward him. No doubt those were the ones who wanted whatever glory lay in being the first to obey the priest's orders. Well and good, thought Blade. Let them win all the glory they want. And he stepped forward to meet them.

He was up with the first man while the other's eyes were still widening in surprise. Then the eyes went blank and closed forever as Blade's sword slashed down through a pitifully clumsy guard, deep into the man's neck. His head dangling on one side, he fell. Blade sprang forward, over the spreading pool of blood, feinted with his sword at the second man, then chopped his left arm off with the axe. The man screamed and reeled back, raising his spouting arm high. Several of his fellows found the sound and sight too much for their fragile new courage, and backed away. The priest's angry shouts rose higher still, and Blade could now make out his words.

"You are picked warriors sworn to serve Ayocan, sworn to obey his priests. But one man stands against you. One man, who has polluted the sacred shores and broken the trees of life and death and slain your comrades among the Holy Warriors! One man, who will make a mighty sacrifice to Ayocan!"

The priest's words made Blade understand his situation better but like it much less. So they were going to sacrifice him to Ayocan—whoever or whatever that was. Did that mean they were going to try to capture him alive? Possibly, but he couldn't count on it.

Those thoughts ran through his mind in seconds and left him clear-headed and alert, ready to continue his attack. The warriors who had been backing away from around him stopped at the priest's words. But Blade was upon them before they could get up the nerve to launch their own attack.

He broke their line by throwing his axe again. This time his target got his sword up in time. The axe struck the bronze blade with a terrific clang, glanced off, sailed into the air, and smashed into a priest's face. Not the chief priest's, unfortunately, only one of his underlings. The man screamed and collapsed, clawing at his smashed and bloody face. The chief priest gave a scream of quite another kind and jumped up and down in a burst of rage.

"Take him, you pigs! Take him, you turtle turds! Take him, take him, take him!" The man's face was dark with fury. For a moment Blade wondered if he were going to fall down in a fit.

But the chief priest did not fall down. Then the warriors attacked and Blade had no more attention to spare for the man. The warrior that had deflected the axe came at him, whirling both sword and axe like the arms of a windmill. That was more spectacular than useful. Blade launched a feint at the man's left side, then whipped his own sword high over his head and brought it down on the man's right shoulder. His arm half-severed, the warrior staggered. Once more Blade plucked an axe out of its owner's failing hand. This time he swung it hard to smash in the man's skull.

The man behind the first warrior tried a slash at Blade, but his sword would not reach. Blade's would, and the warrior reeled back, dropping sword and axe and clutching his stomach to keep the gaping wound there from spilling out all his guts. Blade whirled as he heard footsteps behind him, whirled fast enough to deflect a sword blow with his axe and slash his attacker across the chest. The cut was long but not deep enough to kill, and the man kept on coming. His axe whistled down at Blade's head, but Blade's arm came up and smashed the attacker's elbow, so that his hand opened and let the axe fall. A second later Blade's sword slashed again, deep into the man's thigh, and this time he did stop and go down onto the blood-soaked ground.

The extra time taken in killing the last warrior had let several others get around Blade's flanks. He had to back away again. He realized as he did that if these warriors could ever launch a mass rush at him, they would have him. Did they have some tradition of fighting one at a time, or did they want to wear him down and take him alive? Blade hoped it was the second. If they took him prisoner, he could always look for a chance to escape. But that was no reason to not go on making things expensive for them. A quick slash at a warrior who was crowding too close, and another man down with a leg streaming blood. The chief priest howled again.

Slash with the sword, lopping off limbs, opening chests and stomachs. Deflect blows with the axe, or use it to smash skulls and collarbones into bloody fragments. Scream war cries that made some of the enemy stop and stare—stop and stare for a few seconds too long. Hear the chief priests gibbering with rage as the Holy Warriors of Ayocan went down one by one, sometimes two by two, to litter the ground.

Before long Blade could no longer distinguish one exchange of blows from another, or keep track of his opponents. In spite of his iron endurance, his breath was rasping in and out of his sweat-soaked chest. His sword seemed to weigh a hundred pounds and his axe fifty. One man could not kill two hundred, no matter how much better he might be than any one of them. The enemy's warriors saw him beginning to flag and slow, and rushed in, still one or two at a time. They were too bold and Blade was still too fast, and more dead or wounded men joined the ones already on the ground. Blade stood with a circle of dead around him, in some places piled two or three deep. He could not get out of that circle any more, for the Holy Warriors were all around him. But when they tried to get at him, they were slowed by having to climb over the bodies of their comrades. And no matter how little they were slowed, it was still too much. The voice of the hysterical chief priest grew hoarse and raw.

But that voice finally pushed the warriors forward in a mass rush at Blade. So many of them came forward at once that they got in each other's way. Some stumbled over the bodies and Blade slashed at others, but there were still too many of them coming at him. They pressed in around him, now swinging the flats of their swords and axes. This cost them more men as Blade leaped and whirled and struck with the last of his strength. But eventually an axe blow smashed across his right wrist, and his sword slipped out of numb fingers.

Now a warrior rushed in on Blade's disarmed right side before he could shift his axe, and grappled Blade around the waist. Blade had enough strength left to bring his knee up into the man's groin. He screamed and jerked, but clung. Blade raised his left arm, to smash the man down with his axe, but a dozen hands clutched at the raised arm and pulled it down. Blade jerked and kicked and bellowed like a bull. Then an axe head smashed down on his skull, cold and hard and brutal. He sagged back into the arms reaching to grab him and hold him, as everything around him swirled away into blackness.

CHAPTER 4

When Blade awoke, he was lying on his back on a cool damp surface that swayed under him. Above him was solid blackness. For a moment he had the unnerving thought that he had gone blind from the blow on the head. Then he realized that he was lying under a heavy canopy in the bottom of one of the canoes. He could hear the splash-clunk of the paddles and the high sing-song of somebody calling the stroke.

He felt as though he had been run through a cement mixer filled with large rocks. His head ached, his wrists and ankles were bound with rope tied so tight it gouged the flesh, and he had purple bruises and red welts all over his body. He was also still naked. But at least he was alive. The Holy Warriors and priests of Ayocan had captured him, and now they were taking him to be sacrificed to their god.

Several hours passed, with the sound of the paddles and the calling of the stroke continuing without a break. Blade began to feel uncomfortably hungry and thirsty. More hours passed, and then Blade heard the stroke speed up. The motions of the canoe became livelier. In fact, they became so lively that Blade rolled around in the damp wood of the bottom, adding new bruises to the ones from the battle of the night before.

Before he could wonder for very long what was going on, the stroke-caller shouted out a single sharp cry, and the paddles suddenly stopped. A moment later a long rolling, grating sound came from underneath, and the whole

26

canoe shook and vibrated as it ran up on the shore. Blade slid forward on his bare rear end for several feet, ending up with a number of splinters stuck in his skin and his feet sticking out from under the canopy.

Now that they had reached land, Blade suddenly became the center of attention. Half a dozen warriors snatched off the black canopy, grabbed him, and hoisted him out of the canoe. They lowered him onto a litter of dark blue leather slung between heavy carved wooden poles. Then a contingent of priests shouldered their way through the crowd of Holy Warriors and surrounded the litter. At a shouted signal eight of the priests hoisted Blade up on their shoulders and set off at a trot.

Hands and feet still bound, Blade bounced about wildly in the litter. Several times he wondered if he were going to bounce right out and fall to the ground, adding more bruises to his battered frame. But gradually the priests got in step, or perhaps the path smoothed out underfoot. Now Blade was able to get a better look at his surroundings.

All nine canoes were drawn up on another gravel beach, this one at the end of a long, narrow bay. Bay? Blade took a second look. To his left stretched the wide blue horizon of the lake. But to his right the "bay" ran off into the plain in a winding, narrow channel that seemed to go on endlessly until it went out of sight. It looked more like the entrance to a river flowing out of the lake.

The canoes were drawn up at one end of the beach in a close-packed line. The warriors were still climbing out and gathering in ragged clusters at the bow of each canoe. The priests who were not carrying Blade's litter had gathered separately in front of a cluster of low, blue wooden sheds, painted with more white signs. From a hole in the largest shed's roof, a thick column of yellow-orange smoke rose straight into the calm air, pale in the bright daylight.

Blade felt the litter begin to tilt under him again and heard the priests begin to breathe harder. He looked ahead, and saw that they were climbing up the side of a broad conical mound. Although it was made of the same dreary blue-gray earth and stone as the rest of the plain, its regular outlines told Blade that it was artificial. As they climbed higher up its side, Blade could not help being amazed by its size. Five hundred feet wide at the base and at least a hundred feet high from top to bottom. The amount of labor involved in building this thing must have been incredible. He wondered what purpose it served. He could see only a small hut made of stone slabs on top of the mound, hardly large enough to house a self-respecting peasant.

Atop the mound, the priests lowered the litter to the ground and stood unashamedly gasping for breath. One of them went over to the door of the stone hut. A large set of chimes was hanging there, made of slabs of polished stone three feet long and a good six inches thick. The priest picked up a wooden mallet with a padded leather head and began beating out a complicated rhythm on the hanging stones. Blade was surprised to hear the stones giving off a solid reverberating *brrrroooom* when struck, instead of merely a dull clunk.

The priest reached the end of his rhythm and began repeating it. Before he was halfway through the repetition, the door of the hut slid open, the bronze reinforced stone slab rumbling aside on polished bronze runners. Two more priests came out of the hut, blinking like owls as they stepped into the full daylight. Along with the priests came a powerful blast of hot air, laden with a bewildering and disagreeable mixture of odors. Smoke, cooking, rotting garbage, human filth, unknown spices all poured out together, making Blade's nostrils wrinkle in protest and disgust. The priests, however, seemed not to notice it. The eight litter-bearers, who had caught their breaths now, came over to the litter and again hoisted it into the air. As they carried Blade into the hut, he got a better look at the white-painted carvings on its walls. All showed the same thing, in various poses and sizes—the figure of a man, with he head and wings of a bat. Ayocan? thought Blade. Then the smelly darkness inside the hut swallowed him up.

Before Blade's eyes recovered, the litter tipped up violently as the priests plunged down a steep flight of stairs—at such an angle, in fact, that Blade almost sailed right off the litter. He had momentary visions of plummeting down the dark staircase and reaching the bottom long before the priests—and breaking every bone in his body in the process.

They reached the bottom of the stairs safely, just as Blade's eyes adjusted to the dimness around him. The stairs came out into a long vaulted corridor, dimly lit by oil lamps hung on bronze brackets set in the walls. The lamps burned with the now familiar yellow-orange tinge, their oily smoke blackening the stones and adding to the thickness of the air. At intervals along the walls stood reliefs and statues of the man-bat, all painted white.

The priests carried the litter down the corridor at their usual brisk trot, then swung left into a smaller passage and along it. In a few moments they came up to another stone-slab door. This one rumbled open as they approached it, without any signal.

In the section of the warren beyond this door the ceilings were still lower, the light still dimmer, the stonework still blacker with grease and strange hideous molds, and the smells thicker than ever. They were thick enough to make Blade gag, although the priests still seemed to take no notice. And then he stiffened, as his nose detected a fleeting but sinister whiff of an unpleasantly familiar odor.

It was the sap of the bushes by the lake, the sap with its mysterious narcotic properties, the sap of the bushes that the priests of Ayocan had gathered in such numbers. Somewhere in this underground warren it was being stored or used in large amounts. For what? There were any number of things a religious cult might want a narcotic for, some of them almost innocent, many others not at all so. Considering how the priests and warriors of the cult of Ayocan behaved, Blade doubted if their uses for anything or anybody would be very innocent.

There were sounds as well as smells filling this part of

the cult's—temple? headquarters? monastery? Blade didn't know, and wasn't entirely sure he really wanted to know. But he was determined to find out as much as he could, even if he wasn't going to live long enough to get any use out of it. The habit was too deeply ingrained in him by twenty years of Home Dimension field missions and Dimension X trips. And there was always the possibility that he might find out something that would help him live longer.

So he listened carefully to the sounds floating through the smelly darkness, and tried to identify them. The clink of chains, the tramp of guards' feet, the sound of slops being emptied, occasional human voices. Some of the voices were chanting in the familiar rhythm of prayers to Ayocan, some were barking orders—and some were sobbing, moaning, and even screaming in rage or pain or despair. Blade felt a chill at those last sounds. The purposes of the priests of Ayocan definitely did not sound innocent.

Now they were passing doors made of bronze or stout wooden bars instead of stone slabs, with heavy cross-bars and ropes holding them closed. As the priests swept the litter along the corridor, Blade saw what lay behind those doors. Like the screams, the sights gave him an unpleasant chilling sensation.

Men, chained to the walls, but jerking at their chains, staring wide-eyed, drooling and moaning like idiots. Were they idiots, or were they drugged? Other men—no, not quite men, eunuchs, with thick wads of once white bandages showing that they had become eunuchs only recently. Some of them were boys who had never even been men, and now never would be. Still other men, chained only by the leg, screaming and hurling themselves against man-shaped dummies, hitting them, kicking them, slashing them with swords. Some of these last men wore masks that concealed their whole heads, white masks in the shape of a bat's head.

And women. They were the worst. Most of them were young, most of the young ones were at least pretty, but none of them showed any life in their eyes or in the way they sat. Naked and chained, they sat or lay slumped against the wall, eyes staring blankly at nothing. Unlike the men, most of whom were matted with grime and filth, the women were all as clean as new-laid eggs, their hair long and well kept. But their ankles showed the scars of their chains, and some of their backs showed deep, half-healed welts from savage beatings. Blade did not know why the priests of Ayocan saw fit to maintain this private inferno of theirs. But every bit of it that he saw worsened his impression of them.

Finally his bearers came to a portion of the corridor where the ceiling was so low that the damp stones were sailing past only a few inches above Blade's nose. Then they stopped abruptly. There was the sound of a wooden bar clinking against metal. The litter moved forward again a few feet. Finally the priests set it down. Blade managed to move his head enough to realize that he was in a cell, whitewashed floor and ceiling and walls all around him except at the entrance. That entrance was closed by a hinged grill of stout bronze bars.

Seven of the priests hastily backed away from the litter and out through the arched door of the cell. The eighth, obviously as nervous as a snake charmer trying to charm his first snake, bent over the litter. He held a long-bladed bronze knife in his left hand, and with it he attacked the bindings at Blade's wrists and ankles. Eventually the priest worked his way through those bindings. Then quickly he shoved the knife in his belt and sprang back through the door before Blade could move a muscle. The grill swung shut and a stout wooden cross-bar dropped into place with a solid *clunk*.

Blade could not have moved fast even if he had wanted to do anything as foolish as killing the priest. His hands and feet were numb and had begun to turn purple from the hours of being bound. For a few minutes there was nothing he could do except lie on the floor, and grit his teeth at the agony of blood flowing back into his hands and feet.

31

Then cautiously he rose and hobbled over to the door of his cell. No one was guarding it, but after testing the strength of the grill, Blade realized that no one needed to. The grill was strong enough to hold an elephant, let alone him in his present battered condition. Here he was, and here he was going to stay until they let him out—no doubt to be sacrificed to Ayocan. His best—in fact his only— hope of escaping was to wait until he was back on the surface again. Unless they were going to carry out the sacrifice here, in the bowels of the temple mound? That was a thoroughly disagreeable thought, one he put out of his mind as quickly as possible.

CHAPTER 5

Blade's captivity in the temple mound was something of
an anticlimax. He was not promptly rushed out and sacrificed to Ayocan. He was not even carried farther down into
the depths of the temple mound and sacrificed to the bat-
god. After a while he even stopped worrying about the
prospect of being sacrificed, since it was obviously fairly
remote. In fact, he was being treated more like an honored
guest than an intended sacrificial victim. The process reminded Blade so much of fattening an animal for slaughter,
though, that he could not enjoy it very much.

He could not have been in the bare cell for more than an
hour or two when the grill opened and no less than twelve
priests filed in. They brought with them a folding bed with
a straw-filled mattress and several blankets, pillows, rugs
for the floor, gilded bronze buckets for water and wastes,
and one of the largest meals Blade had ever eaten in his
life. A huge bowl of steaming gruel, that tasted like well-
salted oatmeal, with bits of vegetables lurking in it. An
enormous slab of meat dripping with a thick pungent sauce,
more like underdone pork than any other flavor. A crisp
loaf of white bread large enough and nearly tough enough
to use for a shield. Purple, green, and red fruits that tasted
like nothing Blade had ever encountered or imagined, and
three different kinds of cheese. He was able to wash this
down with both beer and wine offered in jeweled bronze
cups so large he had to use both hands to lift them com-
fortably.

He was hungry enough to welcome this meal, with only a

fleeting worry that the method of sacrifice to Ayocan might be poisoning the victim during his "last meal." Since he could not detect with either nose or tongue any trace of the drug in the food, he did full justice to the meal.

That was just as well. All twelve of the priests stood around him as he ate, staring intently at him each time he showed signs of stopping. They seemed to be almost willing him to eat more and more and still more. Blade wondered after a while if they would try to put food in his mouth if he stopped feeding himself. Perhaps Ayocan was a god of gluttony, and men were sacrificed to him by being forced to eat themselves to death? It was a whimsical thought, soon past. But it was obvious to Blade that he was in no danger of starving as long as he was in the hands of the priests of Ayocan.

After the meal, two priests who were obviously doctors examined him carefully. They were as thorough as their primitive instruments and techniques permitted. Allowing for that difference, their examination was almost as complete as the one Blade received each time he returned to Home Dimension.

After the examination, they tied pads of cloth steeped in hot water over his more serious bruises and scrapes. Hot water, and something else—Blade caught a faint scent that reminded him a little of the narcotic sap, but which was obviously not it.

Finally, one of the doctors said, "You will go to the bed, and you will not leave it or touch the healing cloths until we come to see you again. Do you understand?"

Blade nodded.

"That is good. You are a magnificent specimen of a man. The Brothers in charge of the Death-Vowed have had their eyes on you since you came, and with reason. One such as you would send many spirits to Ayocan before he died, more than any other Death-Vowed the Brothers have had, more than any that any Brothers in all the history of the Houses of Ayocan on earth have ever had.

"But the Supreme Brother has given his orders, and he

34

must be obeyed. And no doubt it is his wisdom that speaks. To deny such a strong spirit as yours to the hunger of Ayocan would be displeasing to him. And Ayocan shall not be displeased." The doctor-priest intoned the last sentence like part of a ritual. Then he turned about and led his companion and the rest of the priests out of Blade's cell. Blade watched them go, and barely managed to hold back a yawn until they were gone. Suddenly he felt terribly sleepy. His one desire was to get into the bed, wrap himself in the blankets, and slide down into a long dreamless sleep. This was exactly what he did.

When Blade awoke, he realized that there must have been a sleeping drug in those cloth pads, one absorbed through the skin. He drank deeply from the bucket of water. Then he realized with a start that the bruises and scrapes covered by the pads no longer hurt. This he wanted to check, no matter what the doctors had said about not touching the dressings.

Carefully he undid the bindings and pulled off the pads. The skin underneath each pad was as clear and whole as if it had never been touched. How long had he been alseep? He felt his chin. Less than twelve hours. Of course he tended to heal quickly. But this quickly? It was impossible. Or rather, it would have been impossible without whatever had been in those pads. Whatever it was, it speeded up healing to an almost miraculous degree. There *was* something in this dimension worth bringing back. Frankly, Blade had begun to wonder about that.

He had time to retie the dressings in place before the doctors reappeared. He hadn't retied them very well, but the two priests either didn't notice or didn't care. They spent most of their time examining Blade's injuries in detail, and the rest in feeling his muscles, testing their tone and condition.

"You heal well, as you should," said the older of the two priests. "The tree of life gives strength. This is pleasing to Ayocan. And Ayocan shall be pleased." The two priests conferred in low voices, and then the older one turned back to Blade.

"You are a warrior of your people, are you not?"

"I am." Blade saw no point in denying the obvious.

"That is good. A warrior's spirit is especially strong. But it is stronger if his body is also strong. You will exercise your body from the time the pail is emptied to the time the first meal is brought in. If you do not do so, your spirit will become surrounded by weak flesh. Ayocan will be displeased at that." And the two priests intoned together, "And Ayocan shall not be displeased."

Blade could not keep a grin off his face. The priests took that as indicating acceptance. "Your spirit is already dreaming of the day when it will be free of the flesh, free to nourish mighty Ayocan. That is good. You will be the greatest sacrifice the Supreme Brother has yet offered. *He* will be pleased, as well as Ayocan." Then the two doctors left Blade alone.

Blade's existence settled down to a routine that made it fairly easy to keep track of time. The "day" began with the arrival of a priest to take out the bucket. Blade then set about exercising for the prescribed time, which turned out to be about an hour. He found it amusing that he was being ordered to do the exercises he would have done anyway, even at some risk. He wanted to be in good condition when —and if—the time came for him to escape.

After the exercises came the first meal. It was invariably fruit, cheese, bread, and alternately hot gruel or cold spiced porridge with milk. A long, dreary day, and then dinner. That was always generous, if not quite as monstrous as his first meal in the temple mound. Then a physical examination by the priests, not as thorough as the first one, but careful enough. And then sleep.

On the third "day" they added something new. They sent him a woman, one of the flawlessly clean, blank-eyed creatures he had seen on the way through the corridors. If there had been any life or spirit in her, Blade would have found her highly desirable, for she was a graceful, clean-limbed

36

little blonde. But there was neither life nor spirit in her. Even the erotic motions she went through seemed mechanical and programmed. It was like making love to a robot. If the priest who brought the girl in hadn't hinted that failure would show a weak spirit displeasing to Ayocan, Blade would have failed. He would not have minded demonstrating the strength of his spirit with one normal woman—or two, or half a dozen. But this poor drugged creature could hardly be called a woman. He was glad that no more were brought to his cell.

The "days" passed slowly one by one. Blade used the spoon they gave him with his meals to scratch a mark for each one on the floor under his bed. There were ten marks there on the "morning" the door opened and nine priests filed in. Eight carried another litter. Blade recognized the ninth as the chief priest from the battle by the lake.

The priests put the litter down and picked up the rope, motioning to Blade to lie down so that they could bind him for travel. Blade hesitated for a second. Was this a reasonable chance to escape? He decided against it and lay down on the litter. Even if he wiped out all nine of these priests—and he would dearly love to do something to the chief priest—that wouldn't mean escape. There would be too many Holy Warriors on the surface, and they might even turn loose some of those drugged berserkers in the bat-masks that he had seen.

The priests bore him quickly to the surface and down the mound to the landing on the river. There was a tenth canoe drawn up on the shore now. It was longer than the other nine, with outriggers on each side and a high prow crowned with a blue enameled bat's head. It was painted a brilliant white, and the warriors sitting in it wore nothing but white cloth and leather.

Blade was loaded aboard carefully but quickly, and then the chief priest climbed aboard after him. A Holy Warrior in the bow hauled the anchor aboard, and another in the stern shouted orders. The Holy Warriors along the sides sprang to their places, paddles dug into the water, and the canoe backed off the beach and out into the river.

In midstream it turned downriver, which Blade judged to be approximately to the south. He watched the mound slip out of sight, then tried to make himself as comfortable as the narrow canoe and his bound hands and feet permitted. He suspected that his worst discomfort on this voyage downriver was going to be sheer boredom. But he would just have to resign himself to that.

This turned out to be a good idea. Blade spent five interminable days in the canoe as it glided endlessly, monotonously southward. The cushions in the bottom of the canoe protected his remaining bruises, but nothing could protect his mind from the sheer tedium of lying trussed like a Christmas turkey, unable to even watch the passing scenery very well. As they had done at the temple mound, the priests in the canoe fed him generously, bathed him carefully, and examined him thoroughly every day. But they made camp only well after dark, and they were on the move again well before dawn. Blade had no way of knowing where he was, where he had been, or where he was going. The only clue he had was an occasional reference by one or another of the priests to the "High Sacrifice in Tzakalan."

On the morning of the sixth day, though, he saw tall green trees by the river, swaying in a warm, damp wind. By noon he could hear a distant roar ahead. It grew slowly louder. And an hour after noon the canoe suddenly swerved toward the bank and ran itself solidly aground.

As the warriors lifted Blade from the canoe, he saw why they had stopped. Barely a hundred yards farther on, the river suddenly vanished. Instead of the slowly flowing clear blue water, there was a belt of tumbling, foaming brown. Then nothing—nothing except a solid wall of mist and spray as the river plunged out of sight.

On the bank above where the canoes had grounded was another temple mound, only a quarter the size of the one by the lake. But the warriors who lifted Blade out of the

38

canoe did not turn up the path toward the temple mound. Instead they turned toward the west, and settled down to a steady loping pace. For several hours they jogged briskly along the edge of the cliff. Blade had occasional glimpses out into space, down toward a misty greenness that seemed very far below indeed.

Toward evening they reached a cluster of white-painted wooden buildings perched between the edge of the trees and the edge of the cliff. At the very edge stood an enormous windlass, more than twenty feet long and six or more feet in diameter. Wound around its drum was an equally enormous mass of heavy yellow-orange rope. Beside it stood something that looked like two large wicker baskets set at opposite ends of a light wooden framework.

Blade's mouth opened to ask a question. Then it stayed open as the answer hit him. They were going to *lower* him down the face of the cliff? In those baskets?

Yes. They lifted him from the litter and lowered him into one of the baskets. The chief priest climbed into the other. One of the Holy Warriors looked at the chief priest and said, "Is it safe, this late in the day?"

"The *oranki* have never come forth in this much light, as you should well know. Sakula will be displeased if he—" jerking a thumb at Blade "—is not present for the High Sacrifice in Tzakalan. He would not be happy at having to make do with any lesser spirit."

"Will a day more or less make any difference, Pterin?"

"To Sakula it will. You should know that. Ayocan will also be displeased at such evidence of sloth in his servants. And Ayocan shall not be displeased." That phrase silenced the warrior. He shrugged and turned away, to start shouting orders.

As priests and Holy Warriors ran to take positions on the handles of the windlass, Blade ventured a question. "Oh, warrior, what are oranki?"

The warrior turned back to him and raised an eyebrow. "You are indeed from a far land, that you have never heard of oranki. They are—" a glare from the chief priest Pterin

39

made him hesitate. "Let me say—if you ever see one you will not live long enough to have to worry about what they are." Then he bent over, and with the dagger from his belt cut the bindings on Blade's hands and feet.

Blade stared at him. So did Pterin. "A strong spirit he is, Pterin. I respect strong spirits, as does Ayocan whom I serve."

"You blaspheme, comparing yourself to Ayocan!" Pterin's voice was shrill.

"Perhaps. But what will happen if you are wrong about the oranki, and they take this strong spirit on his way down to the Lower River? Ayocan shall not be displeased." From the expression on his face, Pterin did not at all like having the ritual phrase of the cult used against him. But he kept silent as the Holy Warrior turned hard about and shouted to the men at the windlass:

"Ready to lower away."

Several of the warriors ran forward, picked up the frame with the two baskets, and carried it to the edge of the cliff. Blade managed for the moment to avoid looking down. Then they took the double ends of the main rope and securely tied them to large hooks on the frame. They lowered the main rope into a padded trough. Then, even more carefully, they picked up the basket frame and lowered it over the edge of the cliff. The frame creaked and swung sickeningly for a moment, the rope creaked and tightened. Still Blake managed to avoid looking down.

Then Pterin nodded. And the warrior turned back to the windlass crew and shouted.

"Lower away!"

CHAPTER 6

Again the basket frame swung sickeningly as the wind-lass crew began paying out the rope. Down the side of the cliff it went, down through the damp air. The seamed and scarred blue-gray stone of the cliff face flowed upward past Blade's eyes. Gradually he got used to the swaying, and looked over and down.

He almost wished he hadn't. Blade was no more afraid of heights than he was of anything else. And he had done an impressive amount of mountain climbing, both on missions and for his own amusement. But then he had always been holding on to the solid mountain, using his equipment and his skills against it. He had not been swaying in a basket in the middle of space, held up only by a rope that might break, payed out by men who might not keep their mind on their job. No, he didn't need to worry about lapses on the part of the crew of the windlass. He and Pterin together made too valuable a package for the men on the windlass to become careless. All he had to do was sit tight and wait—and perhaps worry about the oranki, whatever they were.

There was a good mile of empty air between the top of the cliff and the trees below. At the bottom the forest stretched away until it was lost in the fading light, endless miles of green broken only by the faraway glimmer of the river. Lights by the river shone a familiar yellow-orange, and smoke rose from the trees near those lights. Blade narrowed his eyes, trying to make out details. As he did so, a shrill whistling sounded from below, and he heard Pterin gasp and curse under his breath. Blade looked down.

Rising up out of the shadows on broad black wings was —*something*—vast and hideous. It looked like nothing Blade had ever seen in nightmares, and in fact for a moment he could not even get a clear image of it. But then it swept up past the baskets, to swing outward in a great circle, wings stiff, gliding as it stared at its prey.

From wingtip to wingtip it spanned twenty feet, from beak to tail at least ten. Its skin was pebbled and grained like leather, and every inch of it shone as glossy black as if it had been oiled. It showed neither fur nor feathers nor scales. But as its long bony beak opened and shut, it did show a mass of jagged white teeth.

Blade now knew entirely too well why the warrior had predicted death for anyone who saw an orank. They were a thousand feet below the top of the cliff already. The men on top could neither drive away the creature nor haul them up in time for them to avoid its attack. And the only weapon he and Pterin had between them was the priest's ceremonial bronze knife, with a blade perhaps six inches long.

Pterin had that knife out now, and was holding it at arm's length while his lips moved in silent prayer. But Blade noticed that his eyes never left the orank as it swung about them in great circles. There was nothing wrong with Pterin's courage, at least.

The orank's circles were getting wider now. On each one the creature swept a little closer to the men in the baskets. Now Blade was watching it as intently as the priest was. Would it strike blindly, directly at the men? They had the remotest sort of fighting chance if it did that. Or would it have the wit to slash the rope apart, dropping the men helplessly to their death in the jungle below? They were doomed if it did that. They would plummet helplessly down to smash themselves to pulp on the ground, and the orank could feed at leisure on the remains.

At the outermost point of its widest circle, the creature

42

suddenly turned. It turned so sharply that for a moment the great black wings were almost vertical. Above the toothed beak Blade saw two gigantic red eyes glaring at him. Then the orank leveled out and lunged in toward the men in the baskets.

As it turned, Blade braced himself as best he could and raised both hands. It was coming straight at him, beak open, eyes glaring. Now he could hear the beat of the wings and the creature's breathing, smell its breath, rank with filth and decay. It screamed again, and then it was on him.

As the beak drove forward, seeking to snatch his head from his shoulders in a single snap, Blade ducked. The beak swept past him, the savage teeth clicking shut on empty air. As the creature's neck came within range, Blade chopped down hard with the edges of his hands, right hand first, then left. He did not expect to break the foot-thick neck, but he knew the blow would startle a creature that must be expecting a sitting and helpless prey.

It did. The orank let out a scream of surprise and pain, and did a complete somersault in midair. It did not pull out of its dive until it was a hundred feet below the two men. By the time it had circled back for another attack, Blade was ready again. He noticed Pterin looking at him with interest.

The orank made its second lunge. Again Blade ducked, again his hands lashed out in a deadly double stroke with all his enormous strength behind it. The creature's tough hide bruised and scraped Blade's skin, but this time along with the scream Blade heard bone crack. Once more the creature flipped over in midair and dove away, and this time it fell almost five hundred feet before it could recover.

Perhaps he should try to grab the creature's neck the next time, strangle it or break the neck? No, it was too strong for that. It might pull him out of the basket in its final struggles even if he killed it. And then the orank was coming in for the third pass, and Blade crouched ready to meet it.

The orank was in a rage now, and also in pain. It shook its head from side to side as it came in. As the orank lunged, it misjudged the height of the still descending basket. Its darting head shot under the basket, striking it a tremendous blow that nearly jolted Blade over the side. But the shock also brought the orank to a dead stop in midair. For seconds it hung there, pressed hard against the basket.

Those seconds were all Blade needed. His left hand chopped down even harder than before against the vulnerable neck. His right lashed out sideways, against the wing thrust hard against the frame. The wingbone was large, but like that of any flying creature, it was fragile. In both neck and wing Blade felt bone shatter under his blows.

The orank gave its most terrible scream yet, and dropped away, head twisting feebly on its crippled neck, the broken wing trailing as it frantically struggled to stay in the air with the good wing. It kept on dropping, with Blade watching to see if by some miracle it would recover again and return to the attack. It did not. It kept dropping, until it vanished in the mist that was beginning to gather below.

Blade was sitting back in the basket, gasping for breath, when he heard a sudden, unmistakable, *crack* of breaking wood. Moving very gently and cautiously, he turned to look at the frame.

"Damn," he said.

Both of the poles of the frame were cracked where the orank's wing had struck them. In the fast-vanishing light Blade could not see how bad the breaks were, but he knew one thing. His life and Pterin's depended on their remaining motionless.

"Pterin," he called across to the man in the other basket.

"Yes, warrior—indeed you are a strong spirit, and—"

"Never mind the compliments. The frame poles are cracked. Don't move. Don't even breathe deeply. How much farther down is it?"

There was a long silence from the other basket, as if Blade's words had struck Pterin dumb. Then the answer came softly, as if the priest were afraid speaking aloud might worsen the creaks. "We must be over halfway."

Much good that will do us if the frames break now, thought Blade. When you are falling, a height of two thousand feet is no better than a height of a mile. He took a very shallow breath and gently shifted to a more comfortable position in the cramped basket. Then he settled down to wait. There was nothing else to do.

They were plunging downward at more than two hundred feet a minute. At that rate it would take another ten minutes or more for them to reach the bottom. Would the frame hold together that long? On the other hand, would going down faster increase the swinging motion, increase the strain, increase the risk of that final fatal break? Blade wished he knew. He also wished there was some way to get word up to the crew of the windlass now so far above.

Now they seemed to be going down faster. Had the windlass crew seen another orank, or were they just afraid of one? Well, so was Blade. Another attack was the last thing the battered frame could stand. And falling down through many hundreds of feet of damp twilight to go *splat* on the floor of a forest in some strange dimension seemed a silly way to go.

Less than a thousand feet to go now. They were definitely sinking faster. But the frame was swinging back and forth like a pendulum now, and the more rope above it the wider the swing. Blade found himself having to hold on to the frame to keep from being pitched out, listening to the ominous creakings, listening for the one final *crack* that would hurl him out into space and down.

It did not come. They passed five hundred feet, and Blade saw color returning to the priest's face. The pendulum motion was easing too. The sheer weight of the rope now payed out was beginning to hold them steady, perhaps. Blade hoped so. But his ears were still listening for that sound that would quite literally be the crack of doom.

Four hundred feet, three hundred, two hundred. Blade found he could breathe normally, and unclench hands that had been clamped to the frame like steel claws. Another minute or so, and they would be safe. The descent was slowing now as the windlass crew eased off in paying out the rope. Blade took a deep breath and let it out in a sigh.

Cr-r-raaaak!

Blade felt the basket lurch and sag. He did not need to look at the frame to know what had happened. Instead he looked down. In the darkness it was hard to be sure—but did he see water glimmering faintly below? He had barely time for a flash of hope, when the frames parted entirely and his basket plunged downward.

As it did so, it turned over, throwing Blade out. For a moment he was head down and certain he was going to fall into water. But would it be deep enough to break his fall from nearly two hundred feet up? As these thoughts flashed through his mind, his body was straightening itself. His only hope was to enter the water with his body absolutely straight. Legs went down, head went up, arms went still farther up until they were above his head. Now he was looking up at the sky as the air rushed past, the approaching water below, just enough time to wonder if the cloudy dark sky above would be the last sight in his life—

He hit the water with an impact that seemed to break every bone in his body, dislocate every joint, and flay the skin off the dismantled skeleton. The water closed over him. As he sensed its chill, he realized that he was still alive. His body was still straight when it arrowed into the muddy bottom.

He went into the mud up to his knees and felt a terrible suction like an enormous mouth trying to draw him in deeper. He kicked with his feet, churned with his arms, felt foul-smelling debris float up past him from the muck below. Then he broke free. He had one moment of utter certainty that his lungs were going to burst before he reached the air—then his head broke surface.

His lungs filled in one convulsive gasp, and his vision

slowly cleared. As it did so, the surface of the water suddenly lit up, as a dozen men with yellow-orange torches stepped out onto the bank of the pond. One of them shouted, and his arm shot out. Unmistakably, he was pointing at Blade. The others waved their swords and joined their shouts to the first man's.

Blade said "Damn!" a third time. If the banks of the pond had been unguarded, and the road into the forest clear . . . Well, there was nothing to do now but once more await a better opportunity. Taking his own good time, he began to swim slowly toward the bank.

CHAPTER 7

The warriors on guard around the pond promptly bustled Blade off to a small camp in the forest. There he was joined by Pterin, whose basket had not broken free and who had landed safely, if white-knuckled. Both men were examined by a doctor-priest, Blade with particular care. The doctor did not try to hide his surprise and delight that Blade had fallen from a height of nearly two hundred feet and remained unharmed.

"Such a strong spirit," he kept saying. "A spirit such as we have not seen in many, many years. Such a spirit will be pleasing beyond measure to mighty Ayocan. And Ayocan shall be pleased." Blade was getting more than slightly tired of the ritual phrases about pleasing and displeasing Ayocan.

He was found to be in excellent health. So, rather to Blade's regret, was Pterin. After a night in the camp they returned through the forest, back to the bank of the great river. The clouds hung low, hiding the river's mile-high leap down the cliff. Only a patch of mist low down against the blue-gray cliff showed where it lay.

About a mile downriver from the falls the forest path came out onto the river bank. A boat waited, not a canoe this time, but a massive barge with high sides and an even higher cabin in the stern. A tall, stout mast amidships carried a single square blue sail, and from ports in the sides jutted twelve long sweeps. A fearful reek rose from below decks, suggesting a crew of seldom-washed slaves down there manning the sweeps. The hull, decks, and cabin were all painted and well-scrubbed white. On the bluff bow a massive white carving of the man-bat figure of Ayocan jutted out over the water. Here below the falls, in the damp, semitropical forest, the water of the river flowed sluggishly, a dull and dirty brownish-green.

Pterin went aboard the boat, followed by Blade, bound and carried as usual in a litter. They were barely aboard when the Holy Warrior who appeared to be captain started bellowing orders. Thick lines of woven fiber were cast off, the reefs shaken out of the sail, the sweeps run out. The barge moved out into the stream. From below came the sound of a drum beating out a rowing cadence, accompanied by the occasional crackings of a whip.

The river was more than half a mile wide, its banks thickly overgrown with a dozen different kinds of creeper-hung trees, tangles of vines, clumps of bushes—a solid green jungle. But Blade's eyes were probing the greenness nonetheless. The servants of Ayocan had unbound him and left him unbound when they locked the door of the aft cabin on him. The windows of the cabin were closed by bronze bars, of course, but bars could sometimes be worked loose. Then a quarter-mile swim would take him to shore. He could vanish in the pathless jungles before they even noticed he had gone, certainly before they could organize a pursuit.

This wasn't the time, however. He wanted to wait until the boat was passing down an inhabited part of the river. Blade saw no point in escaping only to die in the jungle. He wanted to escape and find people who could help him on his way, far from this land and the priests and Holy Warriors of Ayocan Who Shall Not Be Displeased. To the devil with them! If he had the chance, he was going to displease mighty Ayocan as much as he could, and Pterin could try to square things with their man-bat god.

Blade waited until the next day before he started working on the bronze bars of his windows. He wanted to be sure that he was not being watched too closely. It did not take him long to realize that the warriors on guard aboard this ship were remarkably sloppy in the watch they kept. They brought his meals and his clean bedding regularly, and escorted the doctors in and out. But otherwise they paid no attention to him. It was as if he were shackled to the boat's timbers by an invisible and unbreakable chain they trusted to keep him aboard under any circumstances. Well, they would soon discover the price of that kind of carelessness.

The bronze was cold-worked and tough, but not tough enough to resist Blade's muscles and ingenuity. Before the evening meal arrived, Blade was able to work two of the bars loose at one end. One more, and he could bend out all three and make a gap large enough to slip even his massive body through. He had seen at least one large village and several isolated houses along the bank since breakfast. They were moving along a populated stretch of the river now. So why wait any longer? Wait until after dark, pull the third bar loose, and then swim for it. Blade carefully replaced the two loosened bars so that they looked normal, and settled down to wait for the evening meal.

It came, heavy and steaming hot as usual. He ate as lightly as he could without arousing the suspicions of the watching doctor. He did not want to have to swim and run on a stomach weighted down with the food provided by the cult of Ayocan. But this would be his last meal at the hands of the cult!

The priests took the plates away. Their eyes rested briefly on the mounds of uneaten food, but they said nothing. Alone again, Blade did a quick series of limbering-up exercises. Good. His body was in more than adequate shape for anything it might have to do during the escape. Then he turned toward the window, eyes on the third bar.

He had just taken a firm grip on it when a sudden outburst of noise from outside made him stop and turn around. He did so just in time. The cabin door flew open, and Pterin and two Holy Warriors tramped in.

"Ah, warrior," said Pterin. "There is a matter in hand that I thought you might wish to see."

"What sort of matter?"

"One of the sweep-slaves has rebelled. He struck a Holy Warrior in the service of mighty Ayocan and drew blood. For this he will be punished."

"How?"

"We shall release him from service on this boat."

How was releasing a slave from service a punishment? Blade managed not to stare in confusion at the priest. There was more in this than Pterin's mere words indicated.

"Why do you wish me to see it?"

"It might interest you."

"Perhaps."

"No, certainly." The priest's face and voice hardened. "Now—do you wish to come out or not?" The two warriors put their hands on the hilts of their swords. The verbal fencing was over. This was an order.

Blade followed the priest out on deck. The two Holy Warriors fell in behind him. Blade took careful note of the distance between him and them. If they were even slightly too far away for a quick reaction, he might have a chance. A quick lunge for the railing, then over the side. He had noticed no bows aboard the boat, or anywhere else among the Holy Warriors of Ayocan. Once he was in the river, they could hardly touch him. It would not be as good as a completely secret escape from his cabin window, for the alarm would be up at once, but—

More noise burst up from below, shouts, thumpings, the rattle of chains. The forward hatch flew open, releasing a stench that made Blade gag. Two warriors scrambled up the ladder from the hold, dragging a filthy, gaunt figure. The sweep-slave was naked except for a breechclout, and so weak he could barely stand unaided. But his eyes glared into Pterin's eyes as the priest approached him.

"Slave," said the priest, "you find service in this vessel of the servants of mighty Ayocan displeasing?"

"What d'ye think, ye damned pimp!"

51

"Indeed, I think you find it displeasing. Well, not all of us are made as to serve the god. And Ayocan will have none in his service who find that service a burden to them. He is not a tyrannous god. So I speak for him when I say—you are to be at once released from service on this vessel."

The slave started and jumped as though he had received an electric shock. He stared at Pterin, his eyes wide with dawning hope. His bony and blistered hands began to shake, and tears streamed down his face, cutting small furrows in the coating of filth on it. "Ye'r speaking truth, priest? Truth?"

"The priests of mighty Ayocan do not lie, slave. It is displeasing to the god. And Ayocan shall not be displeased." Pterin nodded to the two Holy Warriors standing on either side of the slave. "Release him from the service of the ship."

The slave was just starting to say, "If ye could land me near—" when the warriors grabbed his arms. They lifted his wasted body completely clear of the deck in one motion, strode to the railing, and lifted him high above that.

Pterin stood watching, a thin smile on his lips. "For in truth I did not lie. Thus do I release you. Go, with the blessing of Ayocan!" The guards gave a tremendous heave, and the slave shot over the railing and into the river below.

His mouth opened as the guards heaved, and a scream of stark raw terror came out as he soared into the air. It cut off in a gurgle and a splash as he struck the water. A moment later another scream split the evening, and then a third, as though the man was being burned alive. Ignoring the warriors behind him, Blade dashed to the railing and stared down into the river.

Not burned alive, but *eaten* alive. The dark water around the man was being churned white by the frantic dartings of dozens of tiny, savage fish. Then it was no longer white, but red with the slave's blood. The man let out another horrible scream, and threw a hand into the air

52

—a hand eaten bare of flesh, with two fish still clinging to the white bones. Another scream, and then the man had nothing left to scream with, as the fish ate out his throat and then his internal organs. For one more moment his head stood out on the red surface of the water, then it sank out of sight.

Blade turned slowly away from the railing. His eyes met Pterin's. The other man smiled again, and there was a tinge of amusement in his voice as he spoke.

"You see, warrior, how thoroughly we release a man who is unwilling to serve mighty Ayocan. Such thoroughness is pleasing to Ayocan. And Ayocan shall be pleased."

Blade's fists clenched and his jaw tightened. If that damned priest says that once more, he thought, I am going to pick him up and throw him after the slave, and be damned to any chances of escape. That sadistic little—!

The priest saw the fury in Blade's eyes and stepped back quickly. All four of the Holy Warriors on deck drew their swords and formed a circle around Blade. For a moment Blade and Pterin glared at each other. Then the priest's eyes dropped, and he jerked a hand toward the cabin door.

The door slammed shut behind Blade and he heard the lock on the bar snap into place. He sat down on the bed, realizing suddenly that he was shaking all over with rage. He sat quietly, taking slow, deep breaths until the shaking stopped, then unclenched his fists. Now his mind began working again.

He was not going to escape from the barge with the river swarming with those little monsters. He would have to wait until they landed at wherever they were going. The place of the High Sacrifice to Ayocan, Tzakalan? Probably.

But he was not going peacefully if he could not escape before the moment of sacrifice. He would take as many of "mighty" Ayocan's servants with him as he could—starting with Pterin.

CHAPTER 8

It took seven days and seven nights of travel down the Low River to reach Tzakalan, capital of the Kingdom of Chiribu. They passed isolated huts perched on poles along the banks, an occasional village, and once a large town with a temple mound outside it and half a dozen boats tied up at its pier. There was remarkably little traffic on the river, but what there was went in stout-sided barges like the one carrying Blade. On this river an upset or leaky boat would be an instant death sentence for anybody in it.

Most of the way, though, Blade saw nothing but the muddy brownish-green of the river and the various shades of green in the forest along its banks. Once more, his worst enemy was sheer boredom—that, and indigestion from eating too much hot heavy food when he didn't really want to.

By evening on the sixth day the scene on the bank was beginning to change. More boats were passing on the river or tied up at solid stone jetties, and there were more and larger houses, many of them with wide areas of cultivated land around them. At intervals there were sizable towns, of perhaps five or ten thousand people, with bustling markets piled high with colorful produce and baskets of squawking fowl. Blade could see no domestic animals larger than goats and dogs—no cattle, no draught animals.

And there was always a temple mound of Ayocan somewhere just outside each town, always visible from the river, always with its priests in their yellow-orange robes scurrying up and down it like ants on an anthill. Blade began to realize just how powerful and widespread the cult of Ayocan was in the whole of Chiribu, if not in this whole dimension. This might well make escaping difficult. Who would want to shelter a fugitive from the powerful—and ruthless—priests of mighty Ayocan? That would certainly be displeasing to Ayocan. And Ayocan shall not be displeased.

All during the seventh day the country grew more and more thickly populated. The towns were closer together and larger, and what space on the banks they did not occupy was taken up by sprawling estates and peasants' fields. Once two large towns on opposite sides of the river were linked by a bridge of old boats, lashed together with a plank walkway laid across them. All the traffic across the bridge was foot traffic, Blade noticed, and all the burdens seemed to go on the backs of men and women, some in chained gangs of slaves, others walking alone and apparently free. Still no domestic animals larger than household pets and fowl. Chiribu seemed to be like one of the civilizations of the American Indians before the arrival of the Europeans.

Two boats in the center of the bridge were untied to create a gap. The cult vessel slipped through the gap and on down the river. By nightfall on the seventh day there were so many boats around them on the river that it was almost like being in a city. Lights, voices, occasionally the sound of drums or flutes came across the water. Blade went to sleep with those in his ears, along with the perpetual creak of the sail and the clunk-clunk of the endlessly moving sweeps.

The next morning they reached Tzakalan.

Blade's first impression was a massive square solidness. The people who built Tzakalan could not build very high—Blade did not find a single building more than three floors tall. But they built solidly, as though they were trying to imitate natural features of the landscape and make their city last as long as the ground it was built on. Every building followed more or less the same square plan, although some had balconies and some had arcades. Every one seemed built of gigantic blocks of the same roughly dressed stone.

If the buildings of Tzakalan lacked grace, they more than made up for it in color. Blue, green, purple, orange, red, yellow (not the yellow-orange of the cult of Ayocan), black, and every possible and impossible shade and variation of them. In the bright sunlight pouring down on the city, the effect was dazzling and dizzying.

The boat was tied up at a small pier painted blue and white, where the men who ran to take the lines wore the dress of Holy Warriors. Even a private dock, thought Blade. The cult of Ayocan is certainly a state within a state. I wonder what the people think of that. If they don't like it . . .

But that was definitely letting his mind run ahead of things. First he had to find a chance to escape, then succeed in escaping, *then* worry about helping these people shake off the cult of Ayocan—if they wanted to. He would have to be careful here. What seemed to him like brutality and cruelty in the cult of Ayocan might be something perfectly reasonable and normal in the eyes of the people here. If he started shooting off his mouth about their pet god, he might find himself slaughtered even faster than the priests could have done, and with less ceremony or chance of escape.

Except that right now his chances of escape from the priests didn't look particularly good, either. The Holy Warriors had him completely surrounded before the boat bumped against the pier—a dozen of them, all with swords and axes drawn. He might free himself, but he was almost certain to be wounded in the attempt. If he were blemished by a wound and recaptured, they would kill him on the spot, not wait anymore to sacrifice him to Ayocan. And if he were wounded, he most likely would be recaptured. Once again this was the wrong time and the wrong place for escape.

They did not bind Blade and carry him along on a

litter this time. Instead they bound his arms behind his back and tied his ankles together with a short hobble of heavy bronze chain. He could walk briskly, but there wasn't any hope of his being able to run fast enough to get away from an old lady with a cane, let alone a dozen Holy Warriors and perhaps the whole population of Tzakalan.

So Pterin and the Holy Warriors escorted Blade through the streets of Tzakalan. The streets were wide and straight. The people flowing up and down them gave way before the little procession and left it a clear path. The civilian population of Tzakalan did not seem much different from the Holy Warriors when seen close up. They were all lean, wiry, with reddish brown skins, large flat noses, and straight black hair. The men wore cotton or linen kilts, the women long, loose sleeveless gowns of the same materials. Both sexes went barefoot, and Blade noticed that none of the men seemed to be armed.

The air in the city was close and heavy after the open river. Smells hung heavy in it—garbage, human and animal wastes, mud, wood smoke, a dozen others, most of them unpleasant. It wasn't quite as bad as the temple mound by the lake or the slave hold of the boat, but Blade found his nose wrinkling nonetheless as they marched him along.

Suddenly it struck him—one more smell, faint under all the others but unmistakable. He had smelled it too many times, in too many strange places after too many acts of violence. Decay—human decay. And the odor was growing stronger.

Ahead was a section of street where the people huddled close to the walls. In the middle of the street was a patch of white, and on the patch something black and sprawling. Blade knew what it was even before the procession took another step toward it.

How long the man had been dead, Blade couldn't be sure. In this damp climate only a little short of being tropical, decay would set in fast. Bloating and darkening were already well advanced. So was the smell. And there was something carved deep into the man's chest. While Pterin stopped the procession and chanted over the body, Blade had a good look at the blood-caked carving. Unmistakably, it was a stylized pair of bat wings.

A sacrifice to Ayocan? Lying here in the public streets, visible to everybody, rotting away in the middle of the capital city of Chiribu? Possibly. Quite possibly. Strange cults conducted strange sacrifices.

There were more bodies as they moved farther up through the streets of Tzakalan, farther away from the river. Some of the other bodies were comparatively fresh, and one must have been lying out only a few hours. It was the body of a young woman. A girl, actually, for she could hardly have been more than fifteen. She was naked, and the bat-wings had been carved into her bare stomach.

The girl's body was the worst sight for Blade, worse even than some of the other bodies that had been lying out for so long that the putrefying flesh had turned black and begun to fall off the bones. There were no insects around any of the bodies, Blade noticed. No doubt the white powder sprinkled about the bodies was to drive them away.

The procession continued on down the street, past markets, through areas where the paint was flaked and peeling from the buildings. Blade's bare feet were beginning to feel sore from walking on the hot pavement.

Eventually they came out on the far side of the city. It was not much of a surprise to Blade that the first thing he saw there was yet another temple mound of Ayocan. It was by far the largest that he had seen, nearly a quarter of a mile wide at the base and more than three hundred feet high. It was completely faced with blue and white stones, and two broad flights of stairs led up to the building at the top. The building itself gleamed a dazzling white in the sun. From its roof a column of familiar yellow-orange smoke rose into the windless air. Beside it stood an enormous square stone block with a tall, carved blue pole at each corner. The block was not only white, it had been polished until it was almost painful to look at.

"Ah, warrior," said Pterin. "Raise your eyes to the Supreme House of Ayocan and consider your spirit rising from it, free to nourish mighty Ayocan. Tomorrow is the High Sacrifice. Tomorrow your spirit shall fly from your body and rise to Ayocan, who will be greatly pleased. And Ayocan shall be pleased."

With a shrug, Blade did Pterin's bidding, looking carefully at the temple mound. But his reasons for doing that were entirely his own. He was fixing in his mind a mental picture of the temple mound and of the area around it. The better the picture, the better his chances of escape. And if there was no escape? Perhaps this huge obscenely swelling mound would be the place of his death. But in that case it would be the same for a good many of the priests and Holy Warriors of Ayocan.

CHAPTER 9

As Pterin had promised, the next morning they led Blade out to be sacrificed.

They had kept him for the night deep within the temple mound, in a richly furnished cell. And the condemned man certainly ate a hearty meal. In fact Blade could hardly do anything else, with the doctors watching him closely for any signs that his spirit was weakening. They also sent a girl in to him after the dinner, one of the drug-ridden puppets. Once more it was all Blade could manage to do what was very obviously his duty.

More than that. His life depended on his continuing to be a strong spirit as the doctor-priests of Ayocan defined it. Otherwise they would not lead him up on the top of the mound the next morning, where he might have room to run and surely would have room to fight. They would put him to death at once in this cell, dark and smelly for all its luxury. And he would not choose to die that way. He would not choose to die at all if possible, but certainly not that way. So he showed the strength of his spirit with the girl, and after that managed a full night of untroubled sleep.

He was fully awake and alert the next morning when they came for him, ready for whatever might promise a chance of escape. The priests offered him the usual massive breakfast, but he refused it. Too full a belly might slow him down. And there might easily be drugs in the food. He could not detect the distinctive smell of the narcotic, but there might be others.

Pterin must have been told of Blade's refusal at once. Within minutes he came storming down the corridor to the cell, four Holy Warriors behind him and fire in his eye. He faced Blade and glared at him.

"Warrior, do you wish your spirit to become weak, so that Ayocan will reject it when it comes before him? To merge with mighty Ayocan gives great joy for all time. But to be rejected by him gives eternal torment. Know you that?"

Blade shrugged. The casualness was assumed, for he knew that this clash of wills with Pterin could be as important as the clash of swords to come. His chances of escape might depend on his winning it. He fixed the priest with a steady stare of his own, and said coldly, "My spirit is so strong that your little bits of food can do nothing for it. And to eat now would in fact weaken that spirit. A warrior of my people must fast before entering a battle, and this moment I call a battle." He wondered if he had let too much slip out. Pterin might find a hidden meaning in the mention of battles.

Apparently Pterin did not. But he had not fired his last shot. "Then if you will take no food, we shall at least give you the Waters of Strength. That you must take before the moment when—"

"I shall take nothing," said Blade coldly. "All would be against the customs of my people. In fact I would prefer to die here and now, and abandon all hope of my spirit joining with Ayocan. I have no faith in your Ayocan so great that it shall make me abandon my own gods and what they ask of me." Again Blade had a chill moment of wondering if he had pushed things too far. Pterin might throw up his hands in disgust and let Blade alone. Or he might throw up his hands in disgust and oblige Blade by killing him on the spot.

Some of the Holy Warriors and lesser priests cried out "Blasphemer!" at Blade. But Pterin said nothing. No doubt he had heard far worse blasphemies from other sacrificial victims. And then he shrugged and motioned to the Holy

61

Warriors. Pterin might be afraid of the wrath of Ayocan if he denied the god such a strong spirit, however stubborn. And he would certainly be afraid of the wrath of the Supreme Brother of the cult, whose wrath could take tangible shape much faster than the wrath of the god.

With their usual vigor the Holy Warriors seized Blade, but this time they did not bind him. They led him out of the cell, through the corridors, and up the stairs to the surface. Sunlight after darkness for so long dazzled Blade's eyes for a moment. When his vision cleared, he saw the temple mound greatly changed from what it had been yesterday.

A crowd of nearly a hundred thousand people completely surrounded the base of the mound. They would have pushed halfway up its sides, except for a solid ring of armed Holy Warriors holding them back. It was a strangely silent crowd, too, more like a crowd of churchgoers than a crowd on a festival day. Well, this was a religious ceremony, after all—whatever Blade might think of the part he was going to play in it.

Atop the mound the huge stone block had been freshly painted and waxed, so that the sun blazed even more blindingly from the glossy whiteness. A tall canopy of dark blue silk now hung from the poles, and each pole also supported a blue and white banner with the bat-wing symbol of Ayocan on it. The banners sagged limply in the hot, still air.

The top of the mound was so packed with Holy Warriors and priests that if anybody had fainted in the heat and the crowding he could not have fallen. In two places, though, tight-knit circles of warriors kept spaces clear. Inside one circle a cluster of naked men and women stood placidly, their dull eyes showing signs of the narcotic Blade was trying to escape. Lesser sacrifices, no doubt, to whet the crowd's appetite for the main course—Blade.

There was no one inside the other circle. Blade looked at it, and Pterin promptly answered his unspoken question. As usual, the chief priest was glad to boast.

"That is the King's Circle. Yes, warrior, King Hurakun himself attends the High Sacrifice, as do the Princes Kenas and Piralu. Piralu is the most faithful in honoring and pleasing Ayocan, but none are ever lacking in reverence for mighty Ayocan." The priest's tone suggested to Blade's trained ear that neither king nor princes had much choice in the matter, if they wished to keep their thrones, titles, and heads. "You have yet further cause for rejoicing. The departure of your spirit gives our King Hurakun the chance to greatly please Ayocan." By a minor miracle the priest did not go on to add the usual ritual phrase, much to Blade's relief.

The wailing of flutes and the roll of drums floated up from the foot of the mound. Blade looked down and saw the crowd making a path for a column of warriors dressed in black from head to foot. In their midst marched a smaller cluster of figures, also dressed in black robes, with black feathers nodding from massive black-enameled head-dresses.

"Behold," said the priest. "The king and princes approach."

The royal party swiftly climbed the mound. At the top their black-clad warriors stopped, and the three men in black robes and headdresses climbed onto the white slabs alone. The priests and Holy Warriors in turn made a path for them, then quickly made a circle around them.

The presence of the king and his warriors was going to be an extra complication in escaping. Blade was beginning to doubt his wisdom in waiting so long for an opportunity. Instead of winding up with the best opportunity, he now thought he might wind up with one of the worst. But now he could be sure there would be no future ones. He would have to make his move soon, or not at all.

That was as far as his thoughts got before the flutes and drums of the priests started up again. To Blade, they seemed to be making a tremendous amount of noise and almost no music at all. Four of the strongest Holy Warriors suddenly darted into the cluster of sacrificial victims and pulled out a young man. He did not struggle or even drag his feet as they hauled him swiftly to the great white stone block and lifted him onto its top. As the Holy Warriors laid the victim down, nine priests stepped forward. Two seized each limb, while the ninth—Pterin—bent down and took a gleaming bronze knife from a niche in the stone. He raised the knife high, making a series of passes over the prone victim's chest. Blade realized that Pterin was sketching out a bat's wings in the air.

Suddenly the knife darted downward, entering the victim's body just below the rib cage. He jerked, but made no cry, although Blade saw his eyes roll up in his head. He was still silent as the priest swiftly disemboweled him, carving his stomach and groin open in the form of a bat's wings. Then Pterin shouted a single harsh syllable. The flutes shrilled, the drums held a long roll, and the whole top of the stone with the body on it suddenly dropped out of sight.

Blade swallowed. The eerie silence as the knife did its work was almost as unnerving as the sacrifice itself. Well, there would be plenty of noise from him when the time came.

The Holy Warriors were dragging another victim forward now, a young woman. She too died in silence, but Blade noticed expressions beginning to appear on the faces of the priests and warriors around him. Blood-lust was beginning to work on them. Let it go on working a little longer, until they were properly distracted, priests and Holy Warriors alike, and then . . .

A third victim, and a fourth. The top of the white rock was now slick with blood. Even the priests were licking their lips now as each new victim came forward. The warriors around Blade were ignoring him now, their eyes fixed entirely on the block.

Then the flutes and drums sounded again in a new rhythm, and the door to the temple tunnels rumbled open. Out from the darkness below came a nightmare figure. It had a man's body, painted from head to foot a glossy white. But on its neck rode a huge bat's head with foot-long ears and glaring red eyes. From its shoulders blue leathery six-foot wings swept backward, bobbing gently as the—thing—walked. At its waist was a broad blue belt, and from the belt hung a long jeweled knife.

Nightmarish as the effect was, it did not bother Blade for very long. Instead, the apparition acted as a signal for him. This must be the Supreme Brother, the chief of the whole cult of Ayocan, and his appearance the signal for the High Sacrifice. Blade's eyes swept in a circle around him. All eyes were on the Supreme Brother. Now!

He took one step backward, then lunged forward. His solid mass of muscle and bone crashed into the two warriors just ahead of him. They lurched forward. They could not go sprawling, because the crowd was too thickly packed. But they smashed hard into the warriors ahead of them, who in turn did the same to those ahead of them, and so on. The shock of Blade's attack ran clear through the crowd, like ripples in water. And as the first two warriors staggered, they opened a gap in the circle around Blade.

He plunged through that gap. As he did, both arms lunged down toward the warriors' belts. His hands snatched their axes free, then swung them hard to either side. Ribs caved in, blood spurted, and this time both warriors did go down. Blade leaped ahead, red with the warriors' blood, eyes blazing, both axes flashing in his hands.

A foolhardy warrior charged him with a sword. Or perhaps the man had been pushed. In any case it made no difference. Blade blocked the sword-stroke with one axe, and smashed the man's throat with the other. Choking, clawing at his smashed windpipe, blood spurting between his fingers, the Holy Warrior reeled backward as far as he could. He tripped over someone's foot and toppled over. Two warriors and three priests went down with him in a tangle of thrashing arms and legs. They were not hurt, and

65

Blade could not for the moment get to them, but they screamed shrilly in panic.

The screams infected everybody with the same panic. In an instant the whole top of the mound was a mass of priests and warriors, shouting, clawing, cursing, kicking, and shoving at each other. In every mind was the same thought—get away from this—monster—in the shape of a man! If Blade had suddenly changed into the true god Ayocan and started feeding on the blood and bodies of the priests and warriors, the panic could not have been greater.

But he still needed to clear a path to the edge of the mound before he could get away. He swung his axe hard at a warrior who blundered within reach, smashing the man's skull like an eggshell. He stamped down on a leg barring his path, feeling bone crack under his foot. As the man screamed and rolled aside, Blade leaped high, came down on somebody's hand, heard another scream, and nearly went sprawling. For a moment he was off balance and vulnerable, but only one warrior noticed it. The man rushed Blade, trying to knock him down by sheer impact. But Blade had one of his axes up to guard, and the man ploughed straight into it. The impact brought him to a halt. Blade swung the other axe, and the man gasped and doubled up as blood gushed from both his mouth and his gaping stomach.

The man fell backward, and suddenly there was a path over his body for another few feet ahead. Blade leaped over the body, crashing into a priest at the end of the path. He did not even bother to kill this man, merely kicked him aside. A warrior who couldn't get out of the way fast enough was a different matter. Blade kicked him, too, then cracked his skull with an axe as the man crumpled. Then he snatched the dying man's sword from his belt, throwing one of the axes into the middle of the crowd. He needed something with a longer reach for the fighting now.

With sword in one hand and axe in the other, he carved

his way through the struggling mass of people. Looking over the heads of the ones nearest him, he could see some of the Holy Warriors beginning to turn, stand, and draw their weapons. The panic was beginning to ebb. If the Holy Warriors could get at him . . . But they were going to have to fight their way through their own people to get to where he was. And he wasn't going to be there when they arrived.

Now only a single pair of Holy Warriors stood between Blade and the edge of the mound. These two did not run, but neither were they very good fighters. They came at him, and as they did, a stumbling priest blundered across their path. For a moment there was a terrible four-man tangle—warriors, priest, and Blade.

Blade recovered first. He slammed the flat of the axe into the priest's kidneys, sending him staggering out of the way. As a line opened up, Blade's sword followed it, straight to the neck of one of the warriors. The reddish-brown skin gaped and blood poured out and sluiced downward, dyeing the blue leather armor. The man faltered and fell against his comrade, immobilizing the other's axe arm. Blade beat down the second man's sword with his own axe, smashing the sword so hard it flew out of the man's hand and down the side of the mound. Then Blade slashed low at the man's legs. A red line opened along his thigh, and he reeled backward. He went over the edge of the mound, lost his balance, fell, and began rolling with a clatter of weapons. Seconds later Blade followed him, leaping out onto the open slope of the mound.

For a moment Blade found it hard to believe that he was out of the deadly press on top of the mound. He kept looking around for men lurching at him or falling under his feet to trip him. But he quickly recovered. Now to get down the slope, through the thin line of Holy Warriors at the botom, and into the crowd.

But now the Holy Warriors at the base of the mound were climbing up toward him, turning their backs on the crowd. Blade could hear a restless rumble of voices from below and see little eddies of movement in the crowd, but they were all unarmed. There was nothing they could do to help him against the Holy Warriors, even if they wanted to. At a single glance Blade counted nearly thirty Holy Warriors climbing toward him, swords and axes drawn. They showed no signs of panic, whatever might be the case behind him.

The last warrior Blade had killed was still holding his axe. Blade sprinted across the slope to the body, snatched up the axe, and thrust it into his belt. Then he ran straight down the slope at the climbing warriors. The advancing line grew irregular and stopped. Obviously the warriors couldn't make up their minds whether to spread out or bunch up. They might not be panic-stricken, but neither did any of them want to wind up facing Blade alone. Before they could decide, Blade was on them.

Thirty feet away he snatched the extra axe from his belt and threw it at the nearest warrior. The man ducked, but not fast enough or low enough. The hatchet smashed into his right shoulder, and his right hand opened and spilled his sword to the stone with a clatter. But the warrior did not give way as Blade had expected. Whether it was courage or paralyzing fear, he stood his ground, his own axe raised. Blade could not charge in at full speed, and did not. He came down on the man at a trot, his sword and axe raised.

As Blade did this, his opponent took two steps forward. Blade's descending sword drove into the man's body, too deeply. He was dead in an instant, but Blade's sword was fixed solidly in his body. Blade barely held onto it as the man went down, tugging and jerking desperately to free it. As he did so, the man's comrades took courage from his sacrifice and rushed in on either side of Blade.

Blade leaped back just in time to keep from being sliced apart by two swords coming in together. But in leaping to save himself, he had to leave his sword behind. Now he faced the warriors crowding around him with only an axe.

Not for long, however. Seeing Blade half-disarmed made some of his enemies overconfident. They came at him in a solid mass, where no one had room to swing a sword or strike with an axe properly. Blade had all the room he needed, to dart forward and strike like a snake with his axe. A man's arm cracked under the blow, a sword fell— and Blade snatched it up as it clattered on the stone. Blade slashed swiftly with his new sword at the legs of one man who was crowding too close. The man screamed and hopped back on one foot, the other a blood-spouting stump, then fell over backward. Two of his comrades fell with him, one rolling away down the slope.

Now Blade was fully armed once more, and both sword and axe flickered and struck out at his enemies. But while he was rearming himself, more of the Holy Warriors had found the chance to close in around him. Now he found himself completely surrounded by fresh opponents. He was more than a match for any one of them, or even any five of them, but there were many more than that. He chopped and slashed and parried, felt his strokes clang off sword blades or chop deep into flesh and bone. But he also felt the tightness in his chest, the sweat pouring in waterfalls down his body, his legs growing rubbery. His arms seemed to be weighted down with stones tied to them, and the sword and the axe seemed to weigh a hundred pounds apice. The sword was losing its edge as well. Bronze could take only so much punishment, and he had given his sword that much and three times more besides. Now its edge was saw-toothed. More often than not it would only wound, not kill. As the Holy Warriors saw that, they regained still more of their courage, and more and more of them crowded closer, even those with open, bleeding wounds.

Blade didn't know at what moment he realized that he wasn't going to get out of this. All he knew was that in one moment he was still looking for a clear path through the warriors, one down the mound and into the crowd. The The next moment he was no longer concerned with that, only with killing as many warriors as possible before they killed him. He had already done much to make this a memorable High Sacrifice for the cult of Ayocan. But he wanted to do a little more if he could.

He no longer took so much care at guarding, preferring to strike even at the risk of being struck. He started taking wounds, small ones mostly, for the Holy Warriors' swords were getting almost as battered as his own. He grinned as he felt the blood trickle down thighs and torso, felt the pouring sweat sting his wounds. Now he was no longer whole and perfect. No matter how strong his spirit might be, his body made him unfit for sacrifice to Ayocan. The whole High Sacrifice would be spoiled. And whether or not Ayocan was displeased, Pterin and the Supreme Brother certainly would be. That was a large consolation.

A shrill noise began to rise around Blade, filling his ears so that he could no longer hear the clang of bronze meeting bronze or his own panting breath. Then with a shock he realized that the shrill noise was the sound of flutes, loudly played and getting closer. With a still greater shock he realized that the Holy Warriors around him were no longer crowding in to strike. He no longer had to raise his sagging arms to guard against their blows or deliver his own. The Holy Warriors had drawn back, and he was standing by himself on the slope of the temple mound. In a wide circle around him the stone was red and slick with blood and littered with maimed or dead men.

He looked to where the flute music was sounding. A solid column of King Hurakun's black-clad warriors was marching around the temple mound toward him, their swords drawn, their musicians marching in the lead. Blade suppressed a groan. So Hurakun's guard was intervening, to curry favor with the cult of Ayocan? Very well, they would find him just as hard to kill as the warriors of the cult had. No, that couldn't be. He was too exhausted, and the heat and the loss of blood were already making him lightheaded. They would have an almost easy kill. Almost.

He dropped his battered sword and started searching the bodies around him for a better one.

He was reaching down to pick one up when the flutes stopped suddenly. Shouts came from the top of the temple mound, and Blade looked toward it. As he did so, a tall figure in black robes and glossy black headdress stepped to the edge of the white slabs, black plumes waving above him. King Hurakun was about to speak.

The king's voice was high-pitched, almost feminine, but it carried—and it carried authority. "In sight of the people of Chiribu, we, Hurakun, King of Chiribu, invoke the Royal Right of Pardon. We invoke it for this man, warrior and formerly prisoner of the cult of Ayocan for the High Sacrifice. We order that he be taken at once to the House of the Pardoned, and there be given all due and proper treatment. Warriors of Hurakun, take the pardoned."

There may have been further explanations. There may have been reactions—anger, amazement, surprise, joy—from both the priests and warriors atop the mound or from the crowd below. Blade didn't hear any of it. As the black-clad warriors turned toward him, his knees gave under him. He was aware of the feel of baking-hot, blood-slick stone against his cheek as he fell. And then he stopped being aware of anything for quite a while.

CHAPTER 10

Blade was back on the cold blue river above the falls, but this time he was sitting up in the canoe, paddling. He was all alone, and suddenly he was at the falls. He paddled frantically, trying to put the canoe ashore. But he wasn't strong enough, and the cloud of mist at the end of the blue water swept closer—closer—closer. Then the mist rose up around him and the outside world disappeared. He should be over the edge now, and falling down a mile to the muddy Low River. But he couldn't see anything, and he had no sensation of falling.

He had just reached the point of being surprised at that, when he realized that he wasn't in a canoe on the river or anywhere else. So there was no reason why he should feel that he was falling, because he wasn't falling at all! This seemed to be a great and momentous discovery, nearly on a level with the theory of relativity. It occupied all his attention as he tried to figure out why it should be that way.

But not for long. He found his ability to concentrate on the problem slipping away. As it did, he became aware of a soft surface under him, cool breezes blowing over him, a familiar smell in his nostrils. *The narcotic!* That recognition woke him up in a hurry.

He was lying naked on a wide mattress supported by a frame of glossy black wood. The bedposts, he noted, were carved in the form of serpents with three jutting horns on their heads. Black as a symbolic color, and three-horned serpents. That sounded almost as familiar as the narcotic. Of course. He was in the House of the Pardoned of the King of Chiribu. The symbolic color was black, and he recalled seeing three-horned serpents on the banners and the shields of the soldiers. In spite of the smell of the narcotic, he was not back in the hands of the cult of Ayocan. He began to look around the room more calmly, no longer expecting things to jump at him from out of the walls.

The room was large, with fresh air and sunlight pouring in through large arches that opened onto a balcony. The walls and ceiling were painted pale green, the floor tiled in black and dark red. Several flowering shrubs stood in bronze pots just outside on the balcony, the smell of their blossoms drifting pleasantly into the room on the breeze.

Looking down at himself, Blade realized that he was swathed almost from neck to groin in bandages and pads soaked in the healing narcotic. At least he hoped it was the healing form of the narcotic and not the mind-destroying one! Since he was under the protection of King Hurakun, he suspected it was the former. There were also bandages wrapped around his legs and arms, even in places he couldn't recall being wounded. The details of the long fight on the mound were coming back to him, but only a little at a time.

Then he heard light, brisk footsteps approaching along the balcony. A loud male voice issued a challenge, and a softer female one replied. Then suddenly a small graceful figure was silhouetted in one of the arches.

Of all the things that he had seen since waking, the girl who came through the arch was the one Blade most wished was real. No—the woman. As she approached, Blade could see the lines at the corners of her eyes and mouth that suggested thirty years, perhaps more. But her figure was arrow-straight and arrow-slim, with pert, high breasts, and the hair drawn tightly back from her brown face was glossy black. She wore a robe of semitransparent silk, and much to Blade's regret she wore under that a pale green embroidered shift.

73

She came over to the bed and stood by its head, looking down at him, a faint smile playing across her neat little mouth. "So, warrior, you are awake. Could you tell me what is your name among your own people, if you have one? Otherwise we shall have to go on calling you merely 'warrior,' as the priests of Ayocan did. We would not do as they do." There was no mistaking the cold contempt and hostility in her voice as she said the last sentence. Blade suddenly realized that none of the colors he had seen in this palace were those of the cult of Ayocan—no white, no dark blue, no yellow-orange.

"My name is Richard Blade," he said slowly. "My own people are called the English."

"I have never heard of them," said the woman. "Are they beyond the mountains?"

For a moment Blade couldn't understand what she meant. Then he realized she must mean the mountains that bordered the high plateau where he had landed. No doubt they marked the limits of the known world for these people.

"Yes, the English live far beyond the mountains."

"How far?"

"Why do you ask that?" Blade countered.

The woman bit her lip and lowered her eyes. Apparently she hadn't expected him to be that much on the alert for trick questions. He could see her debating in her mind how much to tell him.

Finally she bit her lip again and said slowly, "You are the mightiest warrior ever seen in Chiribu or even in Gonsara."

"Gonsara?"

"The kingdom that lies farther down the Great River, farther to the south toward the Dark Sea."

"I see."

The woman went on. "Suppose all the English were like you? A thousand English warriors could sweep away any army we could put in the field against you. Ten thousand could conquer both Chiribu and Gonsara as easily as a farmgirl taking an egg from under a setting hen."

Blade smiled. He like the woman's honesty, and would repay it in kind. "England is so far away that no English army could ever reach Chiribu." Unless and until Lord Leighton worked out the technique of transporting men by the hundreds into Dimension X, that was certainly true enough. "Even if an English army reached the mountains, it could never climb over them. We have sent explorers to those mountains several times, but if any of them reached Chiribu, certainly none of them ever got back to England." That was not strictly true, but it supported his first statement. "I am a much better fighter and warrior than most of the English, in any case." As far as the kind of fighting he would be doing here in Chiribu and elsewhere in this dimension, that was certainly true. There had not been very many people in the Medieval Club when he was at Oxford. And none of those could beat him with any of the Club's weapons—broadsword, axe, mace, morningstar, and so on.

Blade's words seemed to settle the woman's mind. She smiled again. "I thank you, Richard Blade. What you have told me is most welcome. And what you may be able to do for us is even more welcome." She turned to go.

"Wait a minute," said Blade sharply. "I have told you a great deal about the English, and some things about myself. Who are *you*, that you can come into my room and ask me these questions?" He almost added, "And obviously expect an answer," because her cool poise had irritated him almost to that point. Instead he added, "Are you a girl sent to find out if I am a strong spirit, like the girls in the temple mounds of Ayocan?"

The woman stopped dead in her tracks and turned around. To Blade's surprise she did not seem angry. In fact, she was smiling. Then she started to laugh. She laughed so long and so loudly that tears started streaming down her face, and she had to clasp her hands over her stomach. Eventually she had to sit down on the foot of the bed, her laughter finally subsiding into an occasional giggle.

At last she turned back toward Blade, wiped the tears from her eyes, and smiled again. "Richard Blade, English warrior, I think you are not entirely well yet. Otherwise I much doubt if you would have said such a thing." She rose. "You will see me again when you are better. I am the Princess Mirasa, wife to Kenas, First Prince of Chiribu, heir to the Serpent Throne." And she slipped out onto the balcony and was gone before Blade could get his tongue untangled enough to say anything.

He was certainly off to a fine social start in Chiribu, mistaking the Crown Princess for a harlot! Then he also laughed. He remembered what his drill sergeant had always said any time something went embarrassingly wrong during training. "There's worse things as 'appens in war, Mr. Blade!" Besides, the princess was almost certainly right. He was far from well yet, and the wisest thing to do for the moment was to relax and let the healing extract of the "tree of life" do its work on him.

He spent most of the next two days and nights sleeping for long periods and waking for short ones. No one came into the room during any of the waking periods. Gradually he felt the pain of his wounds fading away under the bandages and pads, and knew that the extract was doing its work. The room was cool from the arched doors that let in fresh air without letting in insects. He was not fed, but his water jug was never empty and his bed linen was always fresh.

On the third day an excessively solemn man with a white beard in vivid contrast to his red robes examined Blade from head to toe with tedious thoroughness. The examination made Blade feel like a prize steer being examined before being entered in a livestock competition, but it did assure him that he was recovering well. More than well in fact—the extract seemed to work even faster here than it had in the temple mound. Bringing a sample of it back to Home Dimension would be an epoch-making breakthrough in medicine.

It was two more days after that before anything else happened. During those two days Blade spent less and less time in bed. His wounds were almost healed, leaving behind them unblemished skin where normally there would have been scars. Blade now felt more in need of exercise than of bed rest, so he put himself through an increasingly vigorous program of calisthenics.

He was doing his exercises on the evening of the fifth day, when the tramp of approaching feet sounded on the balcony outside. Six brawny soldiers of King Hurakun's army strode into the room.

"Richard Blade. It is the wish of the Princess Mirasa that you attend dinner in her chambers this night. We have come to take you there." As far as Blade knew, only the Princess Mirasa here in Chiribu knew his name. But he preferred to be on the safe side. He stepped over to the corner of the room, and reached for his sword, axe, and weapons belt. The leader of the soldiers shook his head.

"You will have no need of those."

"Perhaps."

"Do the English trust no one?"

"The English trust as readily as the next man. But no warrior of my people ever goes from his chamber without his weapons. To ask me to do that would be dishonor." He hoped the word "dishonor" would get the message across —try to take my weapons, and I shall fight you.

Apparently there were brains behind the warrior's abrupt manner. He nodded, and Blade picked up his weapons. The soldier held out a kilt-like garment to him, dark green with a gold-embroidered border and a glossy black leather belt set with semiprecious stones. Blade put it on and hooked sword and axe to the belt.

The soldiers seemed to approve of the results, and quickly formed around Blade and led him out of the room. Down a short flight of stairs they went, and then through a lush garden. The odors from the masses of tropical flowers that spread across the ground and climbed up the stone walls and tree trunks were almost overpowering. Birds shot like brightly colored rockets through the treetops with screeches and twitterings. The garden was well guarded. Blade saw three different squads of soldiers as his own escort hustled him along the gravel paths among the trees and bushes.

Finally a silver-gray mass loomed through the trees ahead. "The Palace of the First Prince," said the leader of the soldiers. They led Blade through a low-ceilinged entrance hall and up a dark stairway lit by the anemic glow of rush torches. At the top of the stairway they left him. "The chambers of the princess are beyond," said the leader.

"What of the First Prince?" asked Blade. The leader said nothing, but the look on his face confirmed a suspicion that had been growing in Blade's mind for some time. Without fail, in every dimension, sooner or later he was called in to play stud to some highborn female with an urge she wanted satisfied. He was too much of a romantic to find that sort of thing entirely satisfactory—but he was also too much of a professional to let his inclinations stand in the way of doing what his job required. And if the road to success in this dimension led through Princess Mirasa's bed—well, he would take that road as far as it led.

The room he entered was all shimmering red and bronze —red tiles on the floor, red paint on the ceiling, bronze paneling on the walls. At a low wooden table in the middle of the room sat Princess Mirasa, in a flowing red gown. This one was also semitransparent—and this time Mirasa was not wearing anything under it. Blade had guessed at the grace and beauty of her body the day he first saw her. He was glad that his guess had been correct. Then he realized that he was indicating that gladness in a very direct way.

Fortunately the kilt was loose about his waist, and Mirasa did not notice his reaction to her. Instead her eyes roamed up and down his body like the hands of the surgeon, but not with a clinical air. Definitely not. They came to rest on his belt, with the sword and axe hanging from it. Her eyes widened.

"Did you think you would need *those* weapons tonight, Blade?"

Blade grinned, to show he understood her double meaning, then shrugged. "I have survived many dangers only by having my weapons always close at hand. I could not be sure that your soldiers were not those of the priests of Ayocan in disguise, sent to snatch me away to another sacrifice or some less dignified way of dying."

Mirasa grimaced. "I told them to use your name, Blade, so that you would know that the message was from me. I am the only one in all the Garden of the Kings who knows it."

"Perhaps. But I could not be sure. Secrets have a way of leaking out."

Mirasa looked at him with a new respect. "Indeed they do. And particularly in this garden, with the Second Prince's spies everywhere. You are wise to recognize the fact."

"Warriors of the English have many occasions to deal with secrets, Princess."

"Then you will be even better fitted for the mission King Hurakun has planned for you."

So he was about to be drafted into the service of the King of Chiribu, was he? He could think of a good many worse fates in this dimension, including the one from which Hurakun had rescued him. So far, this was not bad news. But . . .

"What is this mission, Princess?"

"To go down the Great River into Gonsara, and spy on the temples of Ayocan there."

CHAPTER 11

Blade could not help laughing. For the first time in all his travels into Dimension X, he was going to be used as a secret agent—just what he had been in Home Dimension for nearly twenty years! He had been pirate and messiah and soldier and revolutionary in Dimension X, but never what he had been trained to do and had lived by doing.

Then he sobered. After his dealings with the cult of Ayocan, he could and would be a marked man for the priests of the bat-god. They would be looking for him, and if they found him around one of their temple mounds, whether in Chiribu or Gonsara, he might not live long enough to carry out any missions for anybody. He said as much to the princess.

She nodded. "King Hurakun has thought of all these things. But you will be heavily disguised, so that your own mother would not recognize you, let alone a priest of Ayocan."

"My height cannot be disguised. And I have not seen anyone here in Chiribu as tall as I am."

"That is true. But the Gonsarans are tall and bearded, and there are some men in Chiribu of mixed blood. You will be disguised as one of those."

"I speak no Gonsaran, Princess. That will certainly make people suspicious." He was deliberately testing her now, to see how thorough their planning was. With the alterations the computer made in his brain, it was a pointless question. But he was not going to try to explain Lord Leighton's computer to Mirasa!

She passed his test with flying colors. "The Gonsaran language is not so different from that of Chiribu that it is difficult to learn. Particularly for one who speaks the tongue of Chiribu as well as you do. It is interesting that you do that." Blade tensed. Was he going to be asked how he had learned to speak Chiribuan so well? Mirasa was sharp-witted enough to try trapping him that way, he suspected. But she let the matter drop. Instead she said, "You will have some weeks to learn Gonsaran from the best teachers in all of Chiribu."

"Good," said Blade. "I have done this kind of work before, in England. It is dangerous enough at best. And it is foolishly dangerous if the people who send the spy do not prepare him for his journey."

"We are not fools, here in Chiribu," said Mirasa briskly. "And still less so in the Garden of the Kings. There are those who say that the First Prince is a fool, because I am wiser than he. But he follows where I lead, and is it the act of a fool to follow one wiser than himself?"

That question obviously demanded yes as its answer.

"And you are a wise man and a warrior, so mighty that there is nothing like you outside of legend," she went on. "It would be the act of fools to throw you away like a child throws away a toy that it wearies of. No, you will be prepared as well as possible. I, First Princess of Chiribu, swear it. And I will see it done even if I must go openly against Second Prince Piralu."

"Why should the Second Prince Piralu wish to see me thrown away?" asked Blade. Mirasa's swearing to help him was reassuring, but her motives for that were obvious. He badly needed to find out more about the political ins and outs of Chiribu, Gonsara, and the cult of Ayocan.

By good luck he had chosen the right question. The problem now was not getting Mirasa started, but stopping her. The explanations came out in a continuous flood, so fast that Blade could barely make a coherent picture out of them. Eventually he assembled a picture something like this:

The cult of Ayocan, though not the official cult of the Kingdom of Chiribu, was by far the most powerful there. Many adhered to it out of genuine belief, more out of hope of being saved by the doctor-priests and the extract if they became ill, and still more simply out of fear. Few dared speak openly against the cult and its growth. So it had acquired temple mounds in every city and town, masses of priests, and an entire army of Holy Warriors.

Those who did speak out against the cult of Ayocan too openly did not live long. Often they died mysteriously, but some of them were found with the mark of the cult's Death-Vowed killers carved in their bodies. According to the priests of Ayocan, the Death-Vowed were men and women inspired by the god to send spirits up for him to feed on. So the Death-Vowed were sacred, their roamings and killings free and unmolested, and the bodies of their victims left in the street until the "spirits" were released. Hence the bodies with bat-wings carved in their flesh that Blade had seen littering the streets of Tzakalan.

But it was impossible to doubt that in fact the priests of Ayocan controlled the Death-Vowed, sending them out when they wished, against whom they wished, to sow terror and death among any opposition. Such opposition had been either dead or silent now for some years, and the cult had won many highly placed supporters. Not least among those was the Second Prince Piralu. Young, vigorous, handsome, masterful, he was more popular with the people than First Prince Kenas. And many people would not in fact grieve at seeing him become First Prince, in Kenas' place.

Now there was nothing terribly bad or evil about First Prince Kenas (Mirasa's lips curled in a smile as she said that). But he cut no figure as a Prince and heir to the Serpent Throne of Chiribu. He was stout, clumsy, undeniably ugly in face and figure, but he was far from stupid. However, he preferred to use his considerable wits working on jewelry. As a jeweler, he could give lessons to half the masters of the craft in Chiribu. But as a prince, Kenas did not make the best impression on the people of Chiribu. There were already many who said that Piralu would make a better king when Hurakun died. It would not take many more saying this to make the Supreme Brother of Ayocan pass the word to the masters of the Death-Vowed. And then some morning Kenas would be found dead, the batwings carved across his stomach. On that morning, the hopes of Chiribu for escaping from the clutches of Ayocan's servants would vanish.

So much for Chiribu itself. But there was also the Kingdom of Gonsara, some days down the Great River that had linked the two kingdoms since Worlddawn. Since before men could remember, men and goods had traveled up the river from Gonsara to Chiribu, and down it from Chiribu to Gonsara. Both kingdoms were wealthy, each had things for which the other would pay a great price. So there was much commerce, men came and went freely, and for centuries there had been peace between the two kingdoms.

Perhaps there might not have been, in spite of the trade. But the armies of Gonsara depended on cavalry and ox teams. Their horses and oxen sickened and died in their forests of Chiribu. And the armies of Chiribu fought entirely on foot. Their infantry could not stand against horsement in the open plains of Gonsara. So neither could strike into the heart of the other except at the risk of defeat and terrible loss, and both preferred their trade to war.

But now this centuries-old peace was crumbling. During the early years of the reign of King Hurakun, the Supreme Brothers of Ayocan had begun sending missionaries down the river to Gonsara. Their discipline and supposedly virtuous life (again a curled lip) had made a great impression in Gonsara, where a mutitude of mostly corrupt priesthoods squabbled over the allegiance of the people. Bribes —in gold, women, and drugs—had won over some of the local priests and many of the local lords. Soon the cult of Ayocan had a foothold of land and wealth and power in

Gonsara. Among the mass of the people it was cordially hated, but among the elite it had a solid mass of supporters.

Too solid to please the Kings of Gonsara. The Kings of the House of the Red Ox held no priesthoods in high esteem, particularly not foreign ones with mysterious bloody rites and unapproachable temple mounds. Some of their ministers began investigations—and some of them died mysteriously. King Thambral IV began to hold the priests of Ayocan in still less esteem than before. Suspiciously well organized mobs sacked one or two of the temple mounds.

At that point the priests of Ayocan in Chiribu began protesting. They proclaimed in mighty voices that the unbelieving King of Gonsara was persecuting the priests and followers of mighty Ayocan. This, of course, was undeniable. So equally well organized mobs in Chiribu began attacking Gonsaran merchants and travelers. The Gonsarans replied with more attacks on the temples of Ayocan. The priests of Ayocan began to agitate for the stationing of Holy Warriors in the temples of Gonsara. King Thambral refused, not very politely. A delegation of Elder Brothers waited on King Hurakun, demanding that he force Thambral to accept temple garrisons under threat of war. Hurakun refused, trying to be polite but not succeeding very well. He knew perfectly well what game the priests of Ayocan were playing.

Unfortunately, King Thambral did not. He did not accept garrisons for the temples of Ayocan, but he did stop watching them closely. For the moment the danger of war receded, but Hurakun, Mirasa, and their allies knew it would not be for long. To embroil the two kingdoms in a war and then use their network of temples to seize control of the ruins of both—that was the only game the priests of Ayocan could be playing. And they could play it best in the unwatched temples of Ayocan in Gonsara. Drugs, prostitutes, whole armies of the Death-Vowed—no one knew what lay in those temple mounds. And King Thambral no longer seemed to care.

"Doesn't Thambral think the priests are dangerous anymore?" asked Blade.

"Ask of Higher Powers for the workings of the minds of kings," said Mirasa with a shrug. "Like Hurakun, Thambral has reigned long and has greatly loved peace. He would not see his forty years on the throne end with a futile war against Gonsara's great and honored neighbor."

Blade sighed wearily. "I have known such rulers, too many of them." In both Home Dimension and Dimension X, he added mentally. "Can he be moved to action?"

"He must be!" said Mirasa fiercely. "If he does nothing, he will wake one morning to find the Death-Vowed swarming through Gonsara and slaughtering his subjects before his eyes. Then his subjects will fight back and fall on the priests of Ayocan. The High Priests will call on Hurakun to march against Gonsara. He will refuse, and that will be the signal for his death—his and Kenas'. Piralu will rule in Chiribu, the two kingdoms will fall on each other, and Ayocan's priests will rule the ruins of both!"

"So I am to go down the river to Gonsara, and discover what the priests are doing there. What then?"

"Then you find some way of coming before King Thambral and persuading him to move against the temple mounds and the cult of Ayocan."

Blade grinned. "You don't expect much of me, do you? What makes you think I can do that—or can even be trusted to try it?"

Mirasa shrugged. This gesture imparted a most interesting movement to her half-visible breasts. "I would like to believe that you will do it for the love of Chiribu and hatred of Ayocan. But you are not of our people, and I have lived with the deeds of power too long to believe that anyone's motives can be pure. So I will ask you. You are a marked and terrible enemy of Ayocan. How long do you think you can live here in either Chiribu or Gonsara, unless you help us destroy the temple mounds and their priests? It would not matter whether you fled or hid; the Holy Warriors would seek you out and the priests would drag you to the block of sacrifice. You will aid us not only because you love Chiribu, but also because you love your own life."

Blade nodded. He liked Mirasa more and more. Perhaps she lived by and amid intrigue, but she could be honest—disarmingly honest—when she chose. He would have to be even more on guard because of that, however much he liked her.

Before he could think any farther along those lines, she rose and came around the table to stand behind him. Her hands came down and stroked his cheeks lightly. She smiled, this time with no bitterness in the smile. "And perhaps you will aid Chiribu against the priests of Ayocan for love of me also."

Blade's erection, which had quietly expired during the long discussion of politics, came quickly to life again. Mirasa's hands on his face, her firm taut breasts against his back, her perfume in his nostrils—all combined to arouse him instantly, completely. He could have turned in his chair, thrown Mirasa down on the table, and taken her then and there.

But from his experience with women he sensed that Mirasa demanded deference from her lovers, as well as virility. He rose slowly from his chair, feeling Mirasa's fingers trailing down over his chest as he did so. He turned, gently took her by the wrists, then ran his hands up her arms under the sleeves of her robe. His touch was as light as hers, but he saw her mouth open and heard a little gasp. Lovers were few and far between for Mirasa, it seemed, and the fires burning in her were seldom quenched.

Before he could move again, she had seized his hand and was drawing him to the door that loomed beyond the table. Blade was hardly surprised when the room on the other side of the door turned out to be Mirasa's bedchamber. The great bed in the middle of the room was canopied, and hung round with gauzy red curtains.

Mirasa skimmed across the black rug on the floor soundlessly and so fast that her feet hardly seemed to touch the ground. She jerked the bed curtains aside and turned to face Blade. "Ah, Blade," she said, in a voice that was halfway between pleading and passion, "you must be as powerful here as you were fighting the Holy Warriors. Nothing but your best can be enough for me."

A randy princess indeed, thought Blade. A type he knew well. But also a type he had never failed to satisfy. This was not a boast, it was merely a fact stemming from his own vigor.

Mirasa licked her lips. "Your garments, Blade, your garments—off with them! I want to see that magnificent man's-flesh of yours doing what is fit and proper. And I want to *feel* it."

"You will," said Blade. At least he was able to keep his arousal out of his voice.

He stripped off his kilt and let Mirasa's eyes take in his upstanding and engorged phallus. From the way her dark eyes widened, it seemed to pass inspection, and more. He stepped toward her, arms outstretched. She thrust him back, but there was no strength in her pushing. Blade sensed she wanted him to ignore her protests, to literally sweep her off her feet. The time for deference was over.

His powerful hands went down her body and clasped hard under her buttocks. She gasped again as he tightened his fingers, pinching and plucking flesh that was warm and pliant under the thin material of the gown. Then his hands drifted down farther, and suddenly he jerked them up under the gown, clasping her bare thighs.

Mirasa stiffened as though he had given her an electric shock, and gave a little whimper. Her hands rose to the back of his neck and tightened there so hard that for a moment he thought she was going to strangle him. He kept his own hands in place, moving them up the insides of her thighs until he felt her curly dark hair between his fingers. Curly dark hair that was already damp, and became not just damp but sopping wet as his fingers probed and pressed and squeezed. Now Mirasa's eyes were closed tight, her mouth wide open, and her breath coming in short, quick pants.

Then her body was jerking and her eyes rolling up in her head. Blade saw her nipples standing up so hard and far that they thrust out the fabric of the gown. On his still moving hands he felt the sudden outpouring of her spasm, and he heard her sob and whimper.

There was no romance in that kind of desperate hunger in a woman. But it took more than a little lack of romance to impair Blade's abilities in the presence of a woman so fiercely aroused. Much more. He was still solid and rigid as he stripped the gown over Mirasa's head. He ran his fingers over the graceful body now fully revealed, noting the firmness of the flesh, the incredibly few sags and wrinkles to suggest oncoming age, the enormous nipples, engorged almost to blackness and standing up an inch from the tips of her breasts. He raised a hand to one breast, lowered his lips to the other, heard Mirasa give a gasp that was almost a scream. She was going to reach another spasm soon if he kept up his work on her breasts much longer. But he alternated lips and fingers on her breasts until she was shaking like a sapling in a gale. Her hips were going through intricate motions of their own as he lifted her and laid her on the bed. And he was still as firm as ever as he plunged into her.

She began kicking and jerking under him almost from the moment of his first entrance. But her second spasm passed more quickly than her first, and did nothing to slow or stop Blade. He held back nothing, plunging deep into her dripping canal until her pubic hairs and his were tangled together. He withdrew until he was almost free and she was arching her pelvis frantically upward to recapture and retrap the marvelous phallus that had been driving into her. Then he would sink into her again. And as he did so, his lips roamed over her face, and one hand was roaming over her breasts, cupping them, tweaking and caressing the monstrously risen nipples, stroking their upper slopes. She

88

was no longer gasping because she seemed to have no breath left in her body. Instead she made a low, continuous moan.

Blade felt and heard a third spasm building in her, but he also felt the pressures building up in him. He held on, held back, while Mirasa heaved and twisted frantically for a third time. And he held on and held back for a little longer than that. But in the end there was no more holding back. He plunged deeply into her one final time, and then his control broke and he jetted and poured himself hotly, savagely into her. The hot jetting went on and on until Blade could almost feel that all the fluids of his body were pouring into Mirasa, that she was draining him into a husk.

In time it stopped and he lay on top of her, for she did not seem to know or care that much of his weight was on her. It was a long time before she showed any signs of life. But then she did so with explosive fury, hands and lips roaming over his body. Blade said nothing to discourage her, for he sensed it would not be wise.

And in the end it was unnecessary, for these roaming hands and lips had him aroused again quickly. He was able to do all Mirasa wanted a second time. And then a third, and finally, after a very long interval, a fourth. Perhaps Mirasa did not get what she wanted very often, but she certainly knew how to make sure that she got it when she had the chance. Blade was not modest about his virility, but he would never have predicted that he could do all that he did that night. He was drained and limp in more than one part of his body when Mirasa finally kissed him and told him the soldiers were waiting outside to escort him back to the House of the Pardoned.

"Remember, Blade," she cautioned him. "You must not let a word drop of this night." Blade nodded, and Mirasa, seeing that he might misinterpret what she said, continued. "No, it is not that Kenas is jealous. He knows that I take what he cannot give where and when I can, and from whom. As long as I choose men worthy of respect—and of a place in a royal bed—he holds his peace. No, the problem is your mission. You were not supposed to know a thing about it before King Hurakun summoned you. He feared word getting to Prince Piralu. And so do I. What Piralu knows one day, the cult of Ayocan knows the next."

CHAPTER 12

Blade went before King Hurakun two days later, and went down the Great River only two weeks after that. He spent those two weeks as securely locked up as if he had been the Crown Jewels of Chiribu. He passed the time pretending to learn Gonsaran, perfecting his disguise and cover story, and considering what he had heard and seen at the meeting with the King of Chiribu.

The night of that meeting warriors in black escorted him through the dark paths of the Garden of Kings to an underground chamber and left him there. The walls were bare, damp, and moldy, the smell of earth and decay overpowering, and Blade's nerves tight. They had left him his weapons, but here in this chamber the weapons could not keep off his fear of a trap. Suppose the ceiling were lowered on him, or water flooded in from the ponds in the garden—perhaps bearing the hungry little fish with it? Sword and axe could do little in that case. He was not ashamed to give a start when he heard a noise behind him. Nor did he mind sighing with relief when a section of the wall slid aside to admit King Hurakun, First Prince Kenas, and Princess Mirasa. She shot a quick glance at Blade, with nothing in it to show what had passed between them. Then she stepped back and left the floor to her husband and the king.

Hurakun spoke quickly, without either losing or standing on his dignity. After a few sentences Blade realized that he was going to learn nothing tonight that Mirasa had

91

not already told him. So he concentrated on sizing up King Hurakun and his elder son.

They made a marked and rather depressing contrast. Hurakun must have been close to sixty, but there were only a few strands of gray in his black hair and even fewer wrinkles in his dark skin. He carried himself erect, as a man who had once been a warrior and could be one again if need be. The sword and the axe he carried on his belt were gilded and jeweled, but sharp-edged and well balanced.

The First Prince looked like a man who had never been a warrior, and never would or could be one. In fact, he looked more like a middle-aged and unsuccessful bank clerk than a prince of any land. If Blade had not known Princess Mirasa's character and determination, he would have despaired for Chiribu at the sight of the heir to its throne. Kenas sagged everywhere—belly, shoulders, jowls —in spite of being twenty-odd years younger than his father. His eyes were small, piggish, and perpetually inflamed—no doubt from too much sitting by night at his workbench. His efforts to project some sort of proper dignity would have been amusing if they hadn't been so pathetic. Blade didn't know whether he felt more sorry for the Kingdom of Chiribu, doomed to be ruled by Kenas, or for Kenas, doomed to have to rule when he would be far happier as a modest craftsman. *And* with a wife like Princess Mirasa.

But the politics of Chiribu were not Blade's main concern, nor were the domestic arrangements of its royal family. His job lay in the south, in Gonsara. And he remembered one particular thing that Hurakun said, near the end of his briefing.

"King Thambral's queen is his third wife, a woman less than half his age. She is said to have a great influence over him. To gain her ear would be a great victory for you, although I would not be able to suggest ways of doing this." For a moment Hurakun's eyes rested on Princess Mirasa. Blade suspected that the king made no suggestions about ways of gaining the ear of a dissatisfied wife because he wanted to spare his son's feelings. Or perhaps he suspected Blade already knew more than well enough the solution to the problem.

In any case, the possibility of more bedroom politics was very much in Blade's mind as he boarded the ship Lugsa for the trip downriver to Gonsara. It was an ordinary cargo vessel, broad in the beam and bluff at both bow and stern, with two broad sails to help it downstream. It had ports for a dozen sweeps and benches for the slaves to man them, but sweep-slaves were expensive. They would be rented from a Chiribuan factor in a Gonsaran river port when the Lugsa started her return upriver. On the trip downriver their place could be filled by cargo, so that the ship could carry more, and smell vastly sweeter.

When Blade boarded the Lugsa, he was so thoroughly disguised that he suspected Mirasa had been right. His own mother would have had to look at least three times to recognize him. And no casual observer would have ever guessed he was other than what he seemed—a merchant's agent of half-Chiribuan, half-Gonsaran blood, headed downriver on a master's business. His head was shaved to the skin, and his beard and body hair had been tinted black with a long-lasting dye. They had tried to dye his skin as well, but a spectacular purple rash made it obvious that he was allergic to the dye. Hurakun's men had resigned themselves to letting him go with his natural tan. "If you stay dirty enough," one of them suggested helpfully, "nobody will notice."

He also sported intricate black patterns tattooed under both armpits and around his penis. The tattooing had been prolonged and painful. Considerably longer and more nerve-wracking had been the wait to see if the tattooist's needles had been cleaned adequately. Blade had threatened him with blood-curdling tortures if he didn't clean his needles, but he couldn't be sure the man had understood, or obeyed. In spite of their healing drugs, the people in this

93

dimension seemed to have rather rudimentary notions of cleanliness.

Barges manned by teams of slaves towed the Lugsa out into the river's current. Then the crew, naked except for breechcloths, unfurled the two big ribbed sails. They stiffened as they caught the north wind. Blade saw water begin to curl white at the Lugsa's broad bow.

With wind and current both behind her, the ship made good time. Tzakalan was well out of sight behind them by lunchtime. Blade ate the bean soup and coarse bread, drank the sour beer, and stared at the towns passing by on the shore and the other boats on the river.

One boat in particular caught his attention. She was long and narrow, almost like one of the canoes on the Upper River. With six fast-moving oars on each side and four sails on two masts, she swept past the Lugsa. The other boat was also riding high in the water, so she must have been either heading downriver empty—possible but unlikely—or carrying a high-value cargo. Jewels, drugs, goldsmith's work? All of these were articles in the Gonsara-Chiribu trade. In fact, the boat looked too shallow to even have a real cargo hold. Her rowers sat on the open deck, and a number of bundles wrapped in blue and white canvas were piled amidships.

Blue and white! The colors of the cult of Ayocan! Blade started. Was the fast boat carrying a cargo for the cult? Or did she perhaps belong to the cult? And if so, why was she heading downriver at the same time as the Lugsa with Blade on board? Coincidence, or something more? Blade decided to assume it was something more.

The captain of the Lugsa did not know who Blade was or what he was going to do in Gonsara. But he was a trustworthy man, known to hate the cult of Ayocan as much as was prudent. Blade had no hesitation in voicing his suspicions to the captain.

"Indeed," replied the captain. "And I watch her myself. Nothing unusual I see. But warning you give is wise. I have six men on Lugsa to fight if they are needed. But I think Ayocani not become just river pirates."

"Perhaps. But King Hurakun will not give them what they want. Perhaps they are getting desperate."

"Maybe," said the captain. "If so, they maybe have Death-Vowed on board. Can you fight?"

"I can fight well enough in a pinch," said Blade. He hoped he would not have to show off his fighting skills on the voyage downriver. That might reveal his identity.

"Good," said the captain. "I watch for that boat. If she get close, I call you."

Blade nodded. For the moment the suspected boat seemed to be drawing rapidly away from the slower Lugsa. He decided he could go below for the moment.

Within an hour the other boat was out of sight downriver. The Lugsa crept onward at her own more sedate pace. By the time Blade came on deck again it was nearly twilight. Lights twinkled in villages and isolated houses along the shore. Out in the middle of the river there was a breeze to cut the tropical mugginess.

Blade ate his dinner—more bean soup, more bread, more beer that was even worse than what he had drunk at lunch. By the time he had dropped his bowl into the wash-tub by the foremast, the swift tropical night had fallen. The banks no longer showed any lights. Apparently they were passing along an uninhabited stretch of the river. The only sounds were the creak of the slats in the sails, the splash of water at the bow, and an occasional foot thumping down on the planks of the deck.

An insect whined past Blade's ear. He batted at it. When it had whined away into the darkness, he thought he heard another sound, a new one. He held his breath and listened. It was unmistakable now. Off to the left, the splash of water. A large fish jumping? There were no large fish in this river. The little carnivores ruled the murky waters. A local boat on its private occasions? Small boats stayed off the river at night, as far as Blade knew. He found himself gripping the hilt of his sword as he stared into the darkness, trying to pierce it, strip it away from whatever was out there. Was it his imagination, or did he see a pale flicker of bowwave and behind it the even fainter loom of a ship?

The captain came aft, and Blade beckoned to him. His voice a whisper, he said, "I think there's another ship out there."

"Temple boat?"

"Perhaps. Do ordinary boats run without lights along here?"

"Never!" The captain stepped to the cabin doorway, stuck his head inside, and called softly, "Fighters, on deck." Murmurs came back, and the faint clatter of weapons being gathered up.

The captain was just turning back to Blade when the night fell apart. As swift as thought, the low-slung boat lunged out of the darkness. Clawed grappling hooks soared through the air from her decks and dug into the Lugsa's railings. With a grinding crash, the enemy boat came riding up against the Lugsa's port side. Heart-freezing shrill screams sounded above the crash of wood. They were not screams of fear or pain, but of insane fury. And then above the railing, Blade saw six blazing white bat-masks.

He had no time to see more before the Death-Vowed leaped high into the air, screaming again. They rose so high that for a moment Blade wondered if they were going to take off into the sky like real bats. Then with yet more screams they thudded down on the Lugsa's deck.

If Blade had not seen the approaching boat and if the captain had not alerted his fighters, the Death-Vowed would have swept the Lugsa's decks in seconds. The men came down in fighter's crouches, then sprang toward Blade, swords and knives flashing in their white-gloved hands. More chilling screams poured from the mouths of the hideous white masks.

Blade and the captain surged forward to meet the Death-Vowed. Blade's axe split open a mask and the head behind it. Then the Death-Vowed gave a scream of a very differ-

96

ent kind as Blade's sword chopped off his arm. But a cloven skull and a missing arm could not stop the Death-Vowed at once. Legs moving by pure reflex drove him forward still. Blade had to back away to keep from going down under the man's dying lunge. A gap opened between him and the captain.

Two of the Death-Vowed charged into it, and the captain howled in agony as their knives drove into him. One eye gone and a knife sticking in his belly, he reeled back. But sheer courage kept him on his feet. As one of the Death-Vowed closed in, knife raised to carve the sign of Ayocan on the captain's flesh, the captain's teeth closed on the attacker's wrist. The Death-Vowed screamed and jerked his arm back and forth, trying to shake off the dying man's jaws. Then he screamed again as Blade's axe chopped off the arm at the shoulder.

Two of the Death-Vowed down, four to go. But four against one was more than Blade wanted to face, particularly when the four were men with no care for their own lives. Blade knew such were the deadliest possible opponents, willing to die to take you down with them—sworn to do so, in fact. He backed up again. Out of the corner of his eye he saw other figures appearing at the railing. Not Death-Vowed this time, but the regular Holy Warriors of Ayocan. They were going to leap down behind him . . .

They did. But at the same time the armed fighters of the Lugsa's guard swarmed out of the cabin, brandishing their own axes and swords and screaming vengeance for their captain. They hurled themselves at the Holy Warriors so fiercely that the enemy were hurled backward onto the advancing Death-Vowed. Blade was caught in the middle. For a moment he stood there, jammed so tightly among his enemies that he could not strike at them nor they at him.

By sheer strength he pushed the men away, punching and kicking and shoving. A space opened around him, a space large enough for him to use his weapons. A Death-Vowed caught off balance died with Blade's sword chopping his spine in two. He fell to the deck, writhing like a broken-backed snake, stabbing at Blade's legs still, until Blade slammed a foot down on his ribs. There was a crunch and a gasp and a sudden silence.

A Holy Warrior faced Blade next, but not for long. Axes rang against each other's blows. But Blade's sword crashed through the other's guard by brute force and deep into the man's shoulder. The man's sword fell to the deck, the clang lost in the battle roar all around. But he screamed very audibly as Blade ran him through the stomach. Blood spurted, flowing down onto the deck, making the planks slick. For a moment Blade's feet did a frantic dance on the planks as he fought for balance. A dying Death-Vowed blundered against him, and they both went down.

Blade heard the dying enemy's breath hiss inside his mask, felt claw-gloved hands tearing at his own skin. He got a full nelson on the other's neck and heaved. The spine went with a crack, and the thrashing legs and clawing hands went still. Blade started to rise and another body crashed into him. He went back to his knees and twisted about, hands reaching for the new attacker's throat. But the man—a Holy Warrior—was already dead, face split open and an axe embedded in the mass of bloody bone splinters.

Finally Blade did stand up, as he realized that most of the men around him were also dead. Blood, discarded weapons, and splintered bat-masks lay thick on the deck. Alongside the Lugsa the sails of the Ayocan boat still loomed. Without thinking, Blade snatched up an axe and a sword and hurled himself over the railing. He landed on the enemy's deck so hard that for a moment he went to his knees again, and pain stabbed through one ankle.

A Holy Warrior saw Blade, hesitated for a moment, then rushed in. The hestitation was fatal. Blade was ready to meet the attack, and both axe blow and sword swing clanged off his guard. Blade's riposte met no such resistance, and the Warrior's thigh gaped and spurted.

Blade rose, and feet clattered on the deck as the boat's

crew and priests ran hastily aft. He saw them clustered near the stern. And he also saw the dim glow of a brazier by the railing amidships.

Three strides forward, and his sword licked out. The brazier went over, and hot coals went flying. The tinder-dry matting covering the deck blazed in an instant. By the glow of the fire Blade saw the cluster of men aft cringe and stare. One of them moved forward, cautiously holding out a bucket. Blade snatched up an axe from the deck and threw it with deadly accuracy. The man bent over, staring down at the axe embedded in his stomach. The bucket clattered to the deck and emptied itself uselessly around the man's feet. The flames blazed higher, reaching up for the sails. Then the sails themselves burst into orange flame, and Blade knew the enemy ship was doomed.

He turned, and realized with a cold shock that he would be too in a few more seconds. The survivors of the Lugsa's crew were chopping loose the grappling hooks that held the temple boat alongside. A gap was already widening between the two craft. Blade sprang up onto the railing, and stared down at the water below. It was black in the light of the fire, but he could see dartings and splashings as the scent of blood drove the fish wild. Then he tensed his legs and leaped out into space.

For a chilling moment in midair he thought he was going to fall short, to fall into the jaws of the fish. But two of the Lugsa's crewmen saw him coming, and practically snatched him out of the air. All three of them crashed down on the blood-slick deck with a jar that knocked the wind out of Blade. When he got his breath back and stood up, the enemy boat was drifting away into the darkness, a pyramid of fire almost from end to end. The priests and crewmen were still clustered aft but as Blade watched, he saw a white splash by the steering oar. Someone had decided to accept death from the fishes, rather than from the flames. A moment later a gurgling scream floated across the dark water as the fish tore into the man. The screams did not last long—it would be only a matter of seconds before the man had no lungs or throat to scream with.

Blade turned to the men who had caught him. "Thanks. Without you I'd be on the fishes' menu tonight along with those over there."

A man Blade recognized as the Lugsa's mate nodded. "We could not do less for you. You saved us. Ayocan priests not use Death-Vowed on river before this. I do not understand."

"Neither do I," said Blade. "That was why I wanted to destroy the whole boat and its crew, not just beat off the attack. If their first try at river piracy costs them the boat and the crew, they may think twice before making it a habit."

There was another reason, one he could not mention. The attack by the cult boat suggested that someone high in the cult knew of Blade's presence aboard the Lugsa. Perhaps he knew of Blade's mission also, and was sending a warning downriver to the temple mounds of Gonsara. If so, destroying the cult boat and every man aboard it *might* make sure that the Lugsa reached Gonsara before the warning.

CHAPTER 13

Of the Lugsa's crew of fourteen sailors and six fighters, five sailors, including the captain, and three of the fighters were dead. Virtually all the others had been wounded, two of them so severely they died the day after the battle. Short-handed as she was, the Lugsa was in no danger from the river itself. It flowed broad and straight and deep all the way to Gonsara, and even in bad weather it had no winds or waves high enough to endanger a well-built craft like the Lugsa. What Blade feared was another attack by men— either ordinary pirates or another boatload of Warriors and Death-Vowed sent by the cult of Ayocan. With half her crew dead or disabled, the Lugsa could never fight off such an assault.

As it happened, the rest of the voyage down the river was uneventful, unmolested, and more than a little boring. Gradually they passed out of the belt of tropical forest and into a broad river plain. The trees there grew in clusters well back from the river bank, with cultivated fields and white-painted houses spreading along the bank. The air there was even hotter than it had been in the forest belt, but less humid.

On the sixth day they passed into Gonsara itself. For all the peace between the two countries, both sides had forts marking the border on both sides of the river. And the river itself swarmed with the swift-moving patrol craft of both kingdoms. These stopped and inspected ships bound in either direction.

Two Gonsaran officials boarded the Lugsa and listened

to the mate's tale of the battle that had decimated the ship's crew. It was a carefully edited tale, that made no mention of the cult of Ayocan. Blade had thought of giving a full account, to sound out Gonsaran opinions of the cult. But he had decided against it. Even if the officials were against the cult, they might talk about what they heard—and others might listen. The less said about the fate of the cult boat until Blade reached his destination, the better.

The Gonsarans were little shorter than Blade himself, but considerably thinner. Their bony faces were largely hidden behind bushy coal-black beards. How they wore their hair Blade could not tell, since they wore high tight-wound white turbans. They wore black slippers, white pantaloons, and black sashes. A curved short sword and a curved dagger, both in silver sheaths, were stuck into the sashes. The men who rowed their boat were naked except for breechclouts, but carried six-foot spears with barbed bronze points. Altogether the Gonsarans looked to Blade very much like the warrior race they were supposed to be.

On the tenth day they reached Dafar, capital of Gonsara. Sweating gangs of naked slaves drew the Lugsa into a great basin under the eyes of the guards on the city's walls, and moored her to a long brick jetty. At that point the mate ceased to pay any attention to Blade. His orders had been to take this man—supposedly a merchant's agent—down the river to Dafar. He had done so. Now it was time for him to go about his own business—disposing of the Lugsa's cargo, hiring new crewmen and fighters, renting sweep-slaves, paying port fees and customs duties, and the like. He therefore dismissed Blade from his mind and his ship.

Blade went ashore without resentment. From this point he would be on his own in any case. And he already had a plan, one worked out with great care on the journey. It involved a good deal of danger, which didn't bother him. It also involved gambling that what he had been told about Gonsara was largely correct. That did bother him. But he didn't think he had any choice. If the secret of his mission was out—and he had to assume it was—sooner or later another cult ship would come downriver. And then the hunt would be on. He had to move fast, whatever the risks.

Visitors from Chiribu could move about freely in Dafar. No one questioned or challenged Blade as he drifted up the streets from the docks toward the heart of the city. He considered for a moment making his move here, in the dockside quarter. But the streets were narrow and litter-strewn —it would be hard to run. And the nearest temple mound was well over a mile away. Ducking occasional salvos of garbage and bathwater falling from the windows, Blade continued up the hill.

Another half hour of walking brought him to the marketplace. Here there were still too many people and booths around for a clear run. And so many people could easily start a panic, in which many innocent people and perhaps Blade himself could be killed. Neither prospect pleased Blade. He stopped at a booth to buy blue and white chalks, and walked on.

When he reached the next square, he decided that he had finally come to the right place. A continuous ebb and flow of people and wagons passed through the square. There were even more people on the oranate balconies of the buildings surrounding the square. Blade knew that he would have plenty of witnesses. But he would also have plenty of room to run. All four streets leading out of the square were wide, although their paving blocks were cracking. At the end of one of them loomed the familiar blue and white shape of a temple mound of Ayocan. And to his right was a large blank wall.

Blade walked over to the foot of the wall and took out his blue and white chalks. Working quickly, he sketched in white the outline of a man with a bat's head and outspread wings. By the time he had finished that, he heard the unmistakable murmur of voices behind him. For the moment he ignored them. Instead he concentrated on filling in the details of the outline.

The head he colored white, except for the wide-glaring

103

eyes and the mouth, where teeth showed jagged against a blue interior. Then he started working on the wings. Behind him the murmur of voices rose still higher. He heard anger in it, one or two curses, and a distinct "Shame!" He continued to ignore the crowd that must be gathering behind him. He could only hope that none of them would be provoked enough to simply stick a spear into him from behind. He could also hope that none of the priests or votaries of the cult of Ayocan were artists. *He* certainly wasn't. Fortunately Ayocan was ugly enough so that the hideousness of the drawing would be blamed on the god rather than on the artist.

By the time Blade had finished the drawing of Ayocan, the murmurings from behind him suggested an angry crowd of at least two or three hundred people. That would be large enough for his plans. He turned and stared out at the crowd. He noted the men in pantaloons and turbans or breechclouts, the women in pantaloons and embroidered bodices. He also noted the sullen or enraged expressions on numerous faces and the number of drawn swords and upraised spears. Here in Gonsara the people went armed.

For a moment he wasn't sure that he hadn't already gone too far. His eyes roved over the crowd, sizing up its mood. It was threatening, but not yet out of control. Then he looked toward the temple mound, again measuring the distance. He would have a good run if the crowd got completely out of hand.

His eyes fell on the crowd again. He stood silently, fixing them with his stare, until they began to notice it. Gradually the mutterings died away, spear points dropped, and swords slipped back into scabbards. Good. They weren't so likely now to skewer him on the spot. He took a deep breath and began to speak.

"People of Dafar! Behold the image of the great god Ayocan. Behold the image of him who shall come to accept the strong spirits, to feed on them, to be pleased by them! And Ayocan shall be pleased! I—"

"You can go to hell, you priest's pig!" yelled someone.

104

"Not I," shouted Blade. "You, perhaps. You have a weak spirit, to reject the counsel of one who speaks for mighty Ayocan. A weak spirit indeed. Ayocan will never feed on it when he comes. It would displease him. And Ayocan shall not be displeased."

"Who cares about Ayocan?" shouted a woman. "I please myself—"

"I'll help you, dearie," shouted a male voice. There was a general roar of laughter. For a moment Blade wondered if the whole mood of rage he wanted and needed for his plans wasn't slipping away.

Then the woman's voice rose again. "I please myself, I say—and I please myself by doing this to your damned blood-sucking monster-god!" An arm rose above the crowd, and a ripe fruit sailed past Blade's head to splatter on the wall just above Ayocan's head.

For a moment there was silence. Then as if the woman had given a signal, a barrage of fruit and vegetables came hurtling at Blade. He ignored it, raising himself to his full height and bellowing at the top of his lungs:

"You scorn and mock Ayocan, little people, weak spirits! His curse will be on Dafar when the time comes—his final utter curse! This I promise you in his name!"

"Well, I'll promise you *this!*" came a voice shrill with fury. Something small and dark sailed out of the crowd and cracked against the wall. Fragments of stone landed at Blade's feet. One stung his cheek hard enough to draw blood.

It was time to leave. He began sidling to the right. Break through that side of the crowd, and he would have a clear run to the temple mound. Be careful, though. He didn't want to hurt or kill any innocent people—just get them angry and keep them angry long enough for the priests of Ayocan to notice it.

Several more stones smacked the wall behind him. A small one struck him in the ribs, making him wince. He would have a juicy purple mark there tomorrow. He kept on toward the right, one step at a time, ignoring the stones, still shouting curses and threats in Ayocan's name. He had to be careful, though. Make too many threats, and the priests of Ayocan might think him a mere madman instead of a loyal convert.

He was almost at the edge of the crowd before anyone noticed what he was doing. Then several voices rose at once, shrill and fierce.

"He's trying to get away! Stop him!"

"Send *his* spirit up to Ayocan!" somebody else shouted.

"Kill!" issued from a dozen throats.

Blade didn't wait any longer. He plunged forward like a football player heading for the goal, head down and elbows out. The first man who came within range Blade kicked in the knee and punched in the jaw. The impact of Blade's fist catapulted the man into the crowd, knocking down half a dozen people behind him. More surged forward to get at Blade, tripped over the fallen, went down themselves in a hideous tangle of thrashing limbs and screamed curses.

Blade didn't wait for them to untangle. Again he plunged forward ,trying to avoid stepping on any of the fallen. He reached the far side of the tangle, knocked down two more men who rushed at him, snatched up one of their spears, and kept on going. Now people drew back from around him. He had stopped shouting curses. Now he shouted war cries from all the dimensions he had traveled in, waving the spear about as he did so. People continued to draw back from around him. They could have rushed him easily, but the first few to make the attempt certainly would have died. And for the moment no one wanted to be among those few. Blade had the traditional advantage of one man over a mob.

Before any could screw up their courage far enough, Blade broke through to the open. At the far end of the avenue on his right rose the great temple mound. Contemptuously hurling his spear down on the paving stones, he headed down that avenue. With equal contempt, he did

106

not bother looking back. Instead he raised his voice again in a shout.

"I go to the House of Ayocan in Dafar. There those who serve mighty Ayocan are honored. I will watch the god pass his judgment on you when the time comes. And I will laugh at your writhings and screamings and agony when he calls all you weak spirits. Weak, crawling, tiny spirits, that displease him. AND AYOCAN SHALL NOT BE DISPLEASED!" The last words came out in a roar that must have been heard halfway across the city. Then Blade threw back his head and laughed long and loud and harshly.

Curses and screams of rage rose from the mob. So did more stones and fruits. Then the people on the fringes surged forward, drawing swords, raising spears or their bare fists, mouth open wide. Blade did not wait around to observe more. Turning on his heels, he bolted for the temple.

If Blade had simply wanted to outrun the mob, he could have done so almost without working up a sweat. But he didn't want that. He wanted to bring the whole mob up to the temple of Ayocan hard on his heels. He wanted to make his arrival and his pleas for sanctuary in the temple mound as dramatic as possible.

So he reined himself in, throwing occasional glances back over his shoulder to see if the mob was falling too far behind. Some of the women and older men soon dropped out. On the other hand, a cluster of men in the pantaloons and sashes of warriors soon outstripped the rest and came pelting after Blade full tilt. Two of them hurled their spears as they ran. Both came disagreeably close to Blade. He began to weave from side to side as he ran, to make himself a more difficult target.

A couple of hundred people chasing one man through a major street of a major city in broad daylight was bound to attract attention. Blade began to see heads pop out of doors and windows and peer over the rails of balconies. Some threw pots and pieces of furniture at him, others came out to join the chase. Blade sprinted past a large cart

107

drawn by four longhorned cattle. As the mob came up with the cart, the longhorns bolted, and the cart went clattering and banging away down a side street, the driver hanging on for dear life.

Now it was only a few hundred yards to the temple mound. Blade could see figures moving around on the slopes, and entering and leaving the little white hut on top. And he could also see a cluster of white-pantalooned Gonsaran warriors standing at the base of the mound. Would they try to prevent him from taking sanctuary?

A hundred yards to go. The warriors had seen him and his pursuers. They were rising to their feet and spreading out in a line around the base of the temple mound. Damn it, they were going to bar his path! Or were they? Only one way to find out.

He neither stopped nor slowed as he raced up to the waiting line of warriors. He did not even bother looking at them. Instead he ran straight for a gap between two of them, ignoring the men as though they had been invisible. A sword flashed free and started toward him. But before it could complete the swing, he was through the line and scrambling up the slope of the mound.

As he climbed, he began to shout again, "Help me! Help me! I sought to spread the truth of the god Ayocan among the people of Dafar. Now they seek my life. I sought to serve the god, and I had to flee. Give me aid, give me shelter, have mercy on me!"

The priests had seen him now, and several of them were starting down the mound toward him. As they did so, a tremendous uproar rose from behind Blade, at the foot of the mound. He risked stopping for a moment, to turn and look.

The mob had also dashed up to the base of the temple mound without stopping or slowing. By sheer weight of numbers they were forcing the soldiers back. The soldiers all had their swords drawn. But it was obvious they were reluctant to shed the blood of their own people in defense of the cult of Ayocan. Blade wondered if they might not in fact turn and join the mob, regardless of what King Thambral expected them to do. He had mixed feelings about the idea. On the one hand, the mob and the soldiers might join forces, invade and sack the temple mound, drag Blade out, and hang him. This would certainly cause the needed break between King Thambral and the cult of Ayocan.

On the other hand, Blade would be too dead to take any advantage of the situation. And, other things being equal, he preferred to get out of this sort of affair alive. In the boiling mass of people at the base of the mound, he couldn't make out what was happening. He decided the safest thing was to get up the mound as fast as possible.

He was halfway up when the priests came down to meet him. He threw a quick but searching glance at the face of each one, to see if there were any he could recognize— and who might possibly recognize him. But they were all strangers. He knelt and raised his hands in the traditional suppliant's posture. But he didn't want to look or sound too abject. He wanted to impress them as a "strong spirit." Otherwise they would never admit him, except as someone to be turned into one of their mindless slaves.

"Who are you?" said the first priest sharply.

"One who has sought to serve Ayocan, as I have said. I wrought a picture of the god upon a wall in the Square of the Goldsmiths, and sought to preach to the people. But they desecrated the picture, and all but slew me. I have come to you, that I may continue to serve the god."

The priests were silent for a time that seemed endless to Blade. Behind him he heard the continued howls of the mob. Although the priests here would have no Holy Warriors to set on him, they could still get rid of him quite effectively. All they would need to do was send a message to the mob below—"We reject this false servant of our god. Come and punish him as you see fit." That would mean a messy end for Blade.

"You drew a picture?" said the first priest. There was more incredulity in his voice than anything else.

"That is what he said," put in a second priest.

"I heard him," snapped the first priest.

Blade tried to look humble without looking abject. "Have I erred in some way, making a picture of mighty Ayocan?"

"No," said the first priest. "No error. It is just—well, such courage I have heard of, but never seen. To do this in Dafar, the City of the Witless . . . As I said, such courage . . ." His voice trailed off.

"If he is telling the truth," put in a third priest.

"Of course he's telling the truth!" snapped the first priest. "What else could have provoked a mob like that? A picture—a picture of mighty Ayocan. Such a brave man. Such a strong spirit."

"Then will you accept me for the service of the god, the free service?" Blade asked. He managed to sound like a free man who knows his own worth. But his mouth was dry as he waited for an answer.

"How could we do otherwise?" said the first priest. "Ayocan will reward you himself in time. But for the moment we also can reward you by permitting you to enter Ayocan's service. You are welcome, oh, strong spirit." He turned, and motioned toward the top of the mound.

Blade rose and followed the priest, ignoring the howl of fury that went up from the mob as they saw him being given sanctuary. For the moment he was safe. More important, he had entered the service of Ayocan under better auspices than he had expected—or believed possible. Luck and his professional skills together had done the job.

But as he climbed, he could not help thinking of the irony of saving his life by fleeing to the priests of Ayocan. For him, that was rather like escaping from a pack of wolves by jumping into a pit of snakes.

CHAPTER 14

The priests hustled Blade up the mound and down the stairs into it at a run, as if they wanted to get him out of sight as fast as possible. Considering that the mob was still gathered at the foot of the mound, Blade didn't blame the priests at all.

The door to the stairs rumbled shut behind him and the familiar smelly darkness of a temple mound closed around him. The priests kept in a close circle about Blade as they led him down the corridor and down more stairs, deeper into the mound. This did not bother Blade. The priests here looked no more athletically inclined than the ones he had seen in Chiribu. If there were actually none of the Holy Warriors in the Gonsaran temples of Ayocan, he had only the Death-Vowed to fear. And the priests would be reluctant to release those within the temple mound merely to stop an escaping prisoner.

Unless they recognized him. That was the thing Blade knew he had to avoid at all costs. There just might be a priest able to recognize him even through his disguise, and then the game would be up. The cult would take almost any risk to bring down the man who had learned their secrets, slaughtered their Holy Warriors, and then escaped being sacrificed to Ayocan by the intervention of their enemy King Hurakun. Once again the notion that he had possibly fled into a snake pit occurred to Blade. And as the priests led him still farther down, he kept at a peak of alertness. His eyes roamed the shadows, looking for signs of guards, memorizing the way back to the surface.

111

But Isgon, chief priest of the cult of Ayocan in Gonsara, did not remind Blade of a snake. The Elder Brother looked more like an aging hunting dog—a large man for a Chiribuan, graying, flabby in belly and jowls. His voice was vigorous, though.

"I am told by Brothers of this House that you sought to serve mighty Ayocan in the city outside. Is that so?"

"It is, Revered One."

"Tell me how you sought to serve Ayocan. In your own words, mind you. I have heard how it seemed to these Brothers, but not to you."

Blade told his story, putting in every detail he could think of that might impress Isgon. He succeeded in doing so. By the time Blade had finished speaking, Isgon looked nearly as awe-struck as the priests who had first met Blade.

"For this I can and shall call you Brother and one to be blessed by Ayocan at the time of his coming, though you are not as yet a priest of the god." Isgon sat in silence for a moment, chin sunken into his cupped hands. "Is it your wish to become a priest of Ayocan?"

The question was so unexpected that for a moment Blade was at a complete loss for words. Then his mind leaped to the idea of yet another gamble. Mirasa and Hurakun had both said the Gonsarans would not permit the cult to maintain any Holy Warriors in the temple mounds in Gonsara. So the temple mounds there were almost defenseless. They were protected from the wrath of the hostile people by their friends in high places and by the soldiers of a king who might easily turn against them. It would be a miracle if this state of affairs wasn't preying on Isgon's mind to some extent. Perhaps Blade could offer to lighten his burden?

"Revered One, I am ready to become a priest if it is the will of Ayocan. But I have not heard his call in such a manner. It has come to my mind that your temple mounds here in Gonsara perhaps need protection. Suppose the soldiers of King Thambral had not held back the mob that was pursuing me today?" Isgon shuddered. Blade almost grinned. The priest was ready to walk straight into the trap.

"Indeed there is a need for protection for the Houses of Ayocan here in Gonsara," said Isgon. "But what can you do to help us in that?"

"I have traveled in Chiribu," said Blade. "I have watched the sacrifices there. I saw that your priests and temple mounds had soldiers to protect them from those who reject or defy Ayocan."

"They do," said Isgon. "We call them the Holy Warriors of Ayocan. But King Thambral, may Ayocan curse him, will permit us no such protection here in Gonsara, to stand between the houses of the god and the wrath of his people."

"Indeed," said Blade. "This is known to me. But there must be a good number of strong and brave men among those who follow Ayocan here in Gonsara. Perhaps I could take some of the worthiest and most trusted of these men and train them in a warrior's arts. And when they are trained, you will have your own Holy Warriors, and that cursed King Thambral will be none the wiser."

Isgon's face lit up as if Blade had just announced the impending arrival of the god Ayocan himself. He even rubbed his hands together. Then his face sobered. "Are you a warrior, then, that you can train others so?"

"I have followed the warrior's way all my life," said Blade. "When I first heard the call of the god Ayocan, I asked him if I should forswear that way, and don the robes of one of his priests. No, said the god. That is to waste the strong spirit you have fed all the years of your life as a warrior. Come forward, and put your sword into my service, and in time I shall receive your spirit with joy." Speaking of a personal dialogue with the god was another gamble. Blade had overheard hints of such things in the temple mounds of Chiribu during his captivity. But he couldn't be sure if Ayocan was supposed to be the kind of god who appeared and spoke to men.

Apparently Ayocan was. Isgon nodded, with a look of

113

great respect on his face. "You were wise to heed the call of the god, and we honor you for your wisdom as much as for your service this day and on future days. Many who come offering to serve Ayocan do not show this wisdom. They try to force their spirits along paths where they cannot go, and those spirits weaken. At times their spirits weaken so much that they would leave the service of mighty Ayocan if they could. But this we cannot permit." That last sentence was a hint of the iron hand that might be lurking inside Isgon's velvet glove.

He nodded. "Then is it your decision that I may serve Ayocan as I wish, as I have said?"

"Indeed it is," said Isgon. "Long have we wished such a sword as yourself, to wield against the enemies of the god here in Gonsara."

"I will not be your only sword for long," said Blade. "Find me those men that I have described, and there will be many swords to serve Ayocan in Gonsara."

That seemed as good an exit line as any, so Blade turned on his heel and strode toward the door of the chamber. The priests who had been escorting him had to scurry to catch him, losing some of their dignity in the process.

That was entirely all right with Blade. He wanted to get the message across that he stood in awe only of Ayocan, not of his human servants. He wanted to establish himself as a man with his own reputation, his own notions of proper ways to serve the god, and a short way with those who would deny him either. The more thoroughly he could establish that reputation, the more freedom of action he would be likely to have. Of course, he might overreach himself and end by being expelled—or even murdered. But if he didn't have reasonable freedom of movement, he would be unable to carry out his mission.

He snapped himself quickly out of this moment of philosophizing, to realize that the priests were leading him down still another flight of stairs. Familiar smells, now, the smells of the prison corridor, where the Death-Vowed and the temple prostitutes and slaves led their miserable existence. Close-packed and unwashed humanity, rancid cooking oil, smoke, a faint but unmistakable hint of the drugs. The priests led Blade along this corridor at a trot. There were only four of them now. Where had the fifth one gone?

On around a bend and along another corridor on the same level. There were unmistakable doors set in the walls. Blade's suspicions were aroused. It would be comparatively easy for the four priests to fling open one of the doors and shove him into one of the cells behind those doors.

The suspicions probably saved his life. As they were passing one of the doors, it suddenly slid open. Blade sprang back, dropping into fighting stance. But nothing came out. Insead the four priests darted through the doorway into the chamber beyond. The door rumbled shut behind them, and Blade was alone in the corridor. A second later, he heard from ahead in the dimness the unmistakable rumble of another rock-slab door opening. And a further second after that, the terrifying attack screams of the Death-Vowed split the air of the corridor.

The Death-Vowed themselves came hard on the heels of their cries. Blade had just time to notice that none of the four of them were armed. Then he had to spring clear to avoid their claw-gloved hands. He chopped sideways with the edge of his hand at a neck showing under a white mask and drove the man back. But the man stayed on his feet after a blow that would have killed practically any other opponent. Again Blade had to give way, but this time he did so in a leap that carried him out of reach of the Death-Vowed. And this time when they rushed after him, one of them came on a little faster than the other three. A man sworn to die can be careless of his own life—or simply careless.

Blade met that careless leader with a kick to one knee that stopped him in his tracks. His head in its white bat-mask went back, and he screamed in rage and pain. As his head went back, his throat was exposed. Again Blade closed, again the side of his hand chopped, and this time he heard and felt bone shatter under the blow. Choking, clawing at a throat clogged with bone splinters, the Death-Vowed reeled back against his comrades. They swung to either side of him. Now they could come on fast enough to trap Blade between them. And now Blade could also meet them separately.

Once again he took out a knee with a kick. One man disabled, he turned to the second. The man rushed him, Blade went down, rolling on his shoulders and bringing both feet up. His feet smashed into the Death-Vowed's chest. Blade heard the crack of ribs and a moment later the crack of a skull as the man was hurled back against the wall.

Now Blade rolled hard to the left, taking the last attacker's legs out from under him. The man went down and was still struggling to rise when Blade leaped on him and chopped him across the back of the neck. He stopped trying to rise, and a moment later stopped moving at all. The last living Death-Vowed, the one with the smashed knee, was leaning back against the wall. There was no way for his eyes behind the bat-mask to show a plea for the mercy he did not get.

The whole affair could not have lasted more than a minute at the most. Even Blade, accustomed to the deadly speeds of hand-to-hand combat, found that nightmarishly quick. He had barely managed to work up a sweat, but he found his breath coming fast, as much from nervousness as from the physical exertion. If the attack had been treachery by Isgon, something more would surely follow it.

Blade stood there in the dim corridor for another minute, senses alert and muscles ready to respond to any new attack. Then the rumble of the door from the end of the corridor came again, and three figures came out of the shadows toward Blade. It was Isgon, accompanied by two of his assistants.

Blade relaxed—slightly. The smile on Isgon's face at least suggested good will. But it was only a suggestion.

"You are indeed a warrior," said the priest. "I had not

believed that any man could do what you have just done. You have passed the test set for you."

Blade nodded and kept his voice cool. "And if I had not passed the test?"

Isgon shrugged and pointed to the Death-Vowed on the floor by way of an answer. "There was a man who slew many of the Holy Warriors at the last High Sacrifice in Tzakalan. A strong spirit, one Ayocan would have loved. But King Hurakun pardoned the man, so for the moment he is beyond our reach. Did you perhaps in your life as a warrior encounter this man?"

Blade managed to avoid breaking out in a cold sweat while Isgon was saying this. He also kept his eyes fixed on the other's face, once more watching for any signs of hidden motives. He couldn't find any. For the moment he would have to be content with that.

So he shrugged and said, "Not that I know of. There are many strong warriors one meets in a life of war. Some are friends, some are enemies. One cannot remember them all."

"True," said the priest. "But there can be few such as you. If you can teach as few as a hundred men to do half of what you have done here today—well, Ayocan will have here in Gonsara a mighty force of Holy Warriors. A mighty force indeed. Not even the Supreme Brother in Tzakalan will possess or command such a force." There was a glint in Isgon's eyes as he said this. Once more Blade had to fight back a grin. The chief priest was obviously ambitious to make the cult of Ayocan in Gonsara as independent as possible from the Supreme Brother in Chiribu. If Blade could help him in those ambitions, he would be helping to provoke a split in the cult. And "divide and conquer" was a good way of dealing with any enemy in any dimension.

"I will not promise anything for the moment," said Blade quietly. "First I must see what kind of men I will have to train. But I will teach them everything they are able to learn. This I swear by mighty Ayocan and by my own honor as a warrior."

Isgon grinned. "Indeed, and I will not now ask you for more. Come with me, and I will show you to your chambers." The priest turned and motioned Blade to follow him.

Blade did so. But as he did so, he saw a fast-vanishing flicker of movement in the dimness farther down the corridor. It disappeared so quickly and silently that Blade could only make out that it was small, slight, and wearing a dark robe.

A spy? And if so, for whom? Was somebody keeping an eye on Isgon? Somebody higher up in the cult of Ayocan? Blade would not be surprised. Blade knew that if he himself were the Supreme Brother of the cult, he would certainly be keeping a close watch on the Gonsaran temple mounds.

Well, there was nothing he could do about it now. He was committed to aiding Isgon in creating a local force of Holy Warriors. And he was further into the confidence of the local cult than he had ever expected to be. For the time being he would let matters rest there, keeping his eyes and ears open.

CHAPTER 15

Blade had nothing to do for more than a week, except sit in the chamber assigned to him, eat the lavish meals served to him, and plan the best method of teaching the Gonsaran temple mounds' Holy Warriors. He toyed with the idea of picking out some of the best and making them loyal above all to him, but rejected it. Most of the men assigned to him for training would probably be genuine believers in Ayocan—Isgon would see to that. And the Elder Brother would no doubt also have some of these true believers spy on Blade. Isgon might be ambitious, but he would not let his ambitions lead him into carelessness.

At the end of the week the first ten men arrived for training. Blade looked them over, rejected two as unwilling to accept discipline, and agreed to start training the other eight. He asked and received permission to train them in not only the Chiribuan axe and sword, but in the use of the Gonsaran spear. Otherwise they would be at a fatal disadvantage against Gonsaran soldiers, as far as reach went. Blade would not deny any soldier he was training anything that might save the man's life. Besides, it would hardly make much difference what training he gave Isgon's private army.

He threw himself into the training, for it was a job he had done often, enjoyed, and did well, no matter what the circumstances. None of the eight men he was training had any arms training. Most of them had been common laborers. At first they brought nothing to their training but enthusiasm, strong backs, and apparent devotion to Ayocan.

They responded rapidly, however. Within two weeks Blade knew that he could soon turn over to the eight the training of the next batch of recruits. It was a system that he had used before to create an army—or at least a fighting force —out of nothing. Train a handful of men himself, then have each one train another handful, and so on—a pyramid with himself at the peak (or base).

As much as he threw himself into the training, Blade did not forget his real mission. He did indeed keep his eyes and ears open, and by doing so learned a good deal. Some of this merely confirmed what he had already suspected. But some of it was entirely new.

Isgon was indeed ambitious—and not merely for making the Gonsaran temple mounds largely independent of the Supreme Brother in Tzakalan. He wanted to build a base of power from which he could infiltrate the mother cult in Chiribu and eventually achieve his own election as Supreme Brother. He knew of the present Supreme Brother's ambitious plans for embroiling Chiribu and Gonsara in a war of mutual destruction. But what he could not see was why the present Supreme Brother should be the only one to reap that rich harvest.

So Isgon wanted his own force of Holy Warriors. He was already accumulating a considerable force of the Death-Vowed—hence his willingness to expend four of them in testing Blade's qualities as a warrior. But the Death-Vowed were only useful for assassination and sowing terror. A regular and disciplined force of Holy Warriors would be needed to follow behind the Death-Vowed. The Holy Warriors would strike through the chaos the Death-Vowed had created, bringing the cult of Ayocan to power in Gonsara.

That was Isgon's plan. When he had a good force of the Holy Warriors available, he would call up his two hundred-odd Death-Vowed. They would scatter through Dafar, some having specific targets, such as the king, queen, and army commanders, others told only to strike and slay as widely as possible. Chaos among the rulers and terror among the people would follow. There would be frantic efforts to bring soldiers back from the frontiers to deal with the suddenly rampant cult of Ayocan.

But in the meantime Blade's force of Holy Warriors would seize control of Dafar. Messages would go off up the river to Tzakalan, calling for Holy Warriors from the temple mounds of Chiribu. King Hurakun would not dare to stand in the way of their being sent, for the people of Chiribu would tear him apart if he tried to prevent the just punishment of the impious Gonsarans. A steady stream of Holy Warriors would come down the river, and in a few weeks Isgon would rule in Gonsara. Not over its ruins, either, or at least so he hoped. He would be ruling over a largely intact kingdom, its population and wealth available for the cult's use—and for his own use as well. He would be more than an Elder Brother, he would be a king in all but name. And then how could his Brothers in Chiribu refuse to make him the next Supreme Brother of Ayocan?

The plan was breathtakingly bold and full of gambles. In fact, it was hardly short of the schemings of a megalomaniac. But certainly it was a spectacularly attractive alternative to merely sitting and accepting one's status as a poor relation of the mother cult in Chiribu. And it might just possibly work. Even if it failed, many innocent people might die, and much damage would be done. This Blade wanted to prevent if possible. But for the moment—and the moment lasted better than two weeks—he saw no way to do it.

There were no drugs in his food—he checked every bit of food and drink brought to him for the telltale odor. So they trusted him at least that much. But on the other hand, when he had finished his day's work and his evening meal, they locked him firmly in his chamber. It was forbidden, they said, for any person not a Vowed Brother of the House of Ayocan to be at large in the House by night. So Blade had no chances for any of the night-time ramblings that had brought him so much information on other occasions. There was nothing for him to do at night except

121

sleep. And since the day's work was tiring, he usually slept well. But he slept with a knife under his pillow.

One night early in the third week, he was just drifting off to sleep when he heard a faint *click* at the door of his chamber. Instantly he was fully awake and alert. As slowly as a cat stalking a bird, his hand crept under the pillow and grasped the hilt of his knife. Otherwise he moved no part of his body except his eyes, which swung toward the door. It was solid rock like most of the chamber doors in the temple mounds, but so well balanced and greased that it moved almost soundlessly. The faint click came again. Unmistakably, someone was moving the lever that opened the door. And then the door began to slide quietly open.

Blade drew his knife slowly out from under the pillow and held it ready. The door continued to open, until there was a gap wide enough for a man to slip through. In the next moment a dimly seen figure darted through the gap on soundless feet. As it approached the bed, Blade recognized it. It was the same one he had seen slipping away down the corridor into the shadows, the day of his meeting with Isgon. The spy, now turned assassin? Perhaps.

The figure moved silently toward the bed until it was just outside Blade's striking range. Through half-closed eyes he watched it. It was small and slim. Blade wrinkled his nostrils slightly as he caught a new odor in the air. Perfume, cutting through the heavy air of the underground warren. Perfume?

As his brain completed the thought, he moved. A tremendous jerk of thigh and stomach muscles snapped him into a sitting position. At the same time his powerful hands closed on the blanket, whipping it into the air and letting it drop down over the figure. A squeal of dismay came from inside the dark hood as the blanket settled down over it, enveloping it. As the stranger raised futile arms to ward off the blanket, Blade rolled hard out of the bed, landing on the floor with a thud. He kept on rolling, sweeping the figure off its feet. It let out another squeal of dismay and

122

pain as it landed, and still another squeal as Blade's massive body slammed down on it, pinning it to the floor.

Blade jerked the blanket away with one hand while he held his knife to the stranger's throat with the other. "Now, my friend, who are you? And what are you doing slipping into my chamber by night?"

"You're hurting me," was the whimpered reply.

"Yes, and I'll hurt you a damned sight more if you don't tell me who you are."

"What kind of bully are you, anyway?" An aggressive protest.

That question was so unexpected that for a moment Blade couldn't come up with a proper answer. Then he said, "Not a bully. Just a warrior who has lived a long life by being short with people who invade his chambers by night. Now—are you going to answer my questions?"

Silence. Blade sighed wearily and began slitting through the cloth of the hood with his knife. Soon enough the face under the hood was revealed. And then Blade stopped cutting, and stared hard at it.

His visitor was a young woman. The heavy cosmetics worn by Gonsaran women made her seem older. But they did not disguise the firm, smooth curves of cheek and neck. And there were other firm, smooth curves, which Blade's searching fingers detected under the robes. A young woman. Not the likeliest of betrayers or assassins, but a possible one. Blade did not relax his alertness.

"What are you doing?" said the woman. Her voice was sharp now. She had recovered her confidence.

"Finding out if you're armed," replied Blade. His fingers continued their search, slipping down under the neck of the robe. He felt the woman stiffen as his searching fingers brushed across a breast—and he also felt the nipple of the breast stiffen. He looked at her face. Her eyes were wider now, and a small pink tongue crept out to moisten her lips.

"All I have are women's weapons," she said. Her voice was lighter now as she added, "And with those I think I am well equipped."

Blade was well on the way to finding that out for himself. His hands moved on down the woman's body inside the robe. She wore nothing under it, and the satiny skin was smooth and soft under Blade's fingers. They drifted down past the breasts, which were small, almost girlish, but as firm as perfectly ripened fruit. Both nipples were fully erect before Blade left off stroking them.

A slim waist, firm muscles under the skin, with a small navel set neatly in the middle. The woman giggled and wriggled like a happy baby as Blade's fingers probed there. Then he kept on moving. As he did so, the robe began to loosen from the woman's body, and his hands found more room to do their work. As her slim neck and bare shoulders came into view, dark as old honey in the dimness, his hands reached her thighs. She gave a little whimper as he softly worked around from the satiny skin over her hipbone, down to her knee, then bit by bit up the insides of her thighs.

He moved upward inch by inch, and with each inch his fingers moved the woman moved also. At times she writhed back and forth with small moans and gasps, at other times she stiffened and her eyes went blank and hard. In her mind there was obviously something drawing her toward what her body wanted, and something else pulling her back. Perhaps she was a virgin? Perhaps, but she would not be one for long. The call of her body was too insistent for her to deny it, and it was sounding loudly in Blade as well.

But he took his time, gradually stripping the robe off her with one hand while his other roamed up and down her body. Several times she gave little sobs as his moving hand closed on her mound, playing in the thicket of wiry hair that covered it. Twice she tried to clamp her thighs together, to trap the hand that was working at the seat of her passion. Once Blade snatched his hand away just in time, and she clenched her fists and writhed her hips toward him in search of that maddeningly desirable hand. The second time, he let the solid warm flesh of her inner

124

thighs trap his hand, because he felt the hairs between them already dripping wet with her mounting arousal. There was no holding back in her mind any more, only the urgent call of her body to go ahead.

Blade decided it was time for him also to listen to that same call. With his free hand he stripped the robe entirely away. For a moment he let his eyes rove over the naked body on the floor before him, gleaming darkly. Her breasts were as small and perfectly formed and firm as his hands had suggested. Her waist would have been narrow but for a neat little belly-roll, and her thighs were plumply well formed. She made him think of a small but perfectly matured little bird, with just the right amount of flesh in just the right places. As his swollen phallus plunged between her legs, she moaned and heaved her hips upward, spreading her thighs apart. Blade drew his hand free and lifted her onto the bed. She did not move, did not speak a word, made no sounds except more little whimpers.

For Blade there was no reason at all to wait, and every reason imaginable to go on. But he was slow and careful in his movements as he raised himself above her. And he was even slower and more careful as he let himself down into her.

She was indeed a virgin, but would not be for long. There was little resistance as Blade slipped inside her wet vagina, no cries, only a little quivering of the fleshy thighs as he entered. But as he plunged deeper, her legs came up steadily, as though they were attached to balloons, and locked around his back. Her hips began to wriggle and twist back and forth as she tried to lock Blade as deeply as possible inside her.

It was often a chancy business, trying to satisfy a virgin. But not this time. The woman was ready to be satisfied —spectacularly ready. And spectacular, also, in her climaxes. She sobbed and moaned and howled so loudly when the first one tore through her body that Blade nearly lost his erection on the spot, fearing they would be heard all over the temple mound.

But solid stone walls will block even the sounds of a woman half-mad with passion. Blade's instincts told him that the woman was not remotely satisfied. But the sensations tearing through his own groin told him that he was terribly close to his own release. The combination of her tightness and wetness around his large, swollen, fast-stroking member was becoming rapidly more and more unbearable.

But he had always found the strength to keep going on, and he managed to find it again. A second climax tore through the woman beneath him, as her hips slammed upward against his with almost bruising force. Her mouth writhed and poured out fierce animal noises. Then she went limp, as suddenly as a snapped rubber band. In almost the same moment, Blade also went limp, as he flooded and poured and cascaded into her, his wetness and hers now mingling. He very nearly went limp all over and sagged down on her with his full weight. But he managed to roll off, to lie beside her on the bed.

He lay there until his head had cleared. But even before that his eyes were fixed on the woman again, and his reflexes alert for any threat from her. More than one woman had taken advantage of what she had hoped would be a let-down in his alertness at such times, to try to drug or kill him. None of them had succeeded. He didn't want this woman to be the first one.

But she did nothing, and in fact she was probably beyond doing anything. She lay on her back, legs still spread, her limbs still limp. Her mouth sagged open and her eyes stared blankly upward in exhausted satiation. Blade doubted if she could have flogged either her mind or her body to make any move, either to save her own life or to threaten his. But he remained alert.

Gradually life returned to the woman, and her eyes lost their glazed air and focused on Blade. One hand crept out and gently patted his now limp member. Her lips curled in a faint smile.

As long as the woman was in this mood, Blade decided to return to his original question.

"Who are you?"

"My name is Natrila."

"What are you doing in a temple of Ayocan?"

"I—I serve in the temple. I—"

"*I* think you are not telling the truth, Natrila. The women I have seen who serve in the Houses of Ayocan feed on the tree of death. Their eyes are blank, their minds are dull, and they do not throw themselves upon a man the way you did. You are a woman whose mind at least is free. You are *not* a temple servant. So I ask you again—what are you doing in a House of Ayocan? If you do not tell me what you are and what you were doing coming to my chamber, I will call for Isgon. And I will tell him what you have done."

Natrila stiffened suddenly and gave a little gasp of surprise—or fear. But she was still silent. Blade repeated his question. "Natrila, I do not want to hurt you. But I cannot serve mighty Ayocan properly if I do not know what goes on around this House. You must tell me, or I shall speak to Isgon."

Natrila stiffened again, but this time she gave a small snort of defiance. "You want to serve Ayocan properly. Hunh! Do you think that matters to me?"

Blade realized he had accidentally struck a vulnerable spot. But he maintained his severe face and tone. "Perhaps I should also tell Isgon that you do not care for the service of mighty Ayocan. And if you do not, why are you polluting this House of the god with your presence? That must be displeasing to Ayocan. And Ayocan shall not be displeased."

Natrila stared at Blade as though he had suddenly started gibbering and drooling like a madman. "I don't understand you, warrior. I just don't understand you. How could you do what you have just done—so well—and yet believe in that bat-winged bloodsucker Ayocan?"

"You blaspheme!" said Blade sharply. The sharpness

127

he put in his voice was largely to help him keep his face straight. He was finding it harder and harder to present the image of a fanatical warrior-worshiper of the bat-god. But if he let the mask drop even once, the shoe might suddenly be on the other foot. Instead of him threatening to tell Isgon of the woman's behavior, she might then threaten to tell tales of his disloyalty.

Natrila stiffened at the edge in Blade's voice. There was a pleading note in her voice this time as she spoke.

"For the love of whatever gods there are, please don't tell Isgon! He—he would not be pleased at what we have done."

"*Why?*" Blade put ice into that one word.

"Isgon is my father." Natrila sagged down onto the rumpled bed and let her head drop into her hands. Tears glistened in the corners of her eyes. Blade would have liked to be sympathetic, but for the moment he had to press his advantage.

"Your father? How is it that an Elder Brother of the Houses of Ayocan has a daughter? He must have most wickedly violated his obligation to celibacy."

"Oh, the devil take obligations to celibacy and you too! Nine out of ten of the priests of Ayocan stick it into any woman they can catch whenever they can catch her. And then if the woman conceives a child or breathes a word of what happened, the priests send the Death-Vowed out after her. She winds up lying rotting in the street with a bat-wing carved on her guts."

"You will not turn me aside by attacking the sworn serving Brothers of Ayocan! And you have not answered my question. How did your father come to have you—and to keep you here, in the holy House of Ayocan!" Blade found it hard to keep his face and voice under control as he said this. He hoped Natrila would mistake the contortions of his face for an almost uncontrollable rage.

Apparently she did. In a small voice she said, "He is a good man in some ways, for all his ambitions. When my mother said that she was carrying me, he did not send

128

the Death-Vowed out against her. Instead he sent her gold, and told her to raise me until I was eighteen, and then send me to him. She did all this, and I came to him, and here we are. I pass as one of the servants. Only a few of my father's most trusted men know who or what I am."

"Indeed," said Blade, to cover his momentary uncertainty. He was beginning to feel uncomfortable about pushing this wretched girl any further. It took all the detachment he had learned in twenty years in the intelligence business to keep him going. "I can see that he would be displeased to learn what you have done. But I think I can see my way to not telling him."

Natrila raised red eyes to stare at Blade. "You can?"

"Under one condition," went on Blade. "That you tell me what goes on in this House of Ayocan, starting at once. Your father has made me the trainer and leader of his Holy Warriors. But he tells me little or nothing of what I need to know about the Houses of Ayocan in Gonsara, that I may defend them well. If you will tell me what he does not, my mouth remains closed. And perhaps my bed will even remain open to you."

That last offer made Natrila wriggle uncontrollably. "Oh, yes, yes. Please. That was why I came to you. I knew that I was a woman, but my father thought me only a girl. And I would trust none of the other Brothers. But you—you are such a man—and I thought I could trust you—" Her voice broke again.

Blade sat down beside her and held her until she stopped crying. "You can trust me, Natrila, as long as you keep telling me what goes on in the temple mound here." He had to fight back the temptation to tell her what he was really here to do. Certainly she seemed to hate the cult of Ayocan and its priests enough so that she would never deliberately betray him. But there were always slips of the tongue—and there could always be torture.

Eventually Natrila gave Blade the promise he wanted, and slipped out. Alone, Blade sat on the bed, a sour expression on his face. He felt dirty over what he had done

129

to Natrila, as though he had abused a child's trust. And he felt a terrible fury at the cult of Ayocan, that had put him in this position. Natrila's shame was one more thing he would avenge on the cult as thoroughly as possible.

A desire for vengeance was unprofessional, he recalled all his instructors (including J himself) saying over and over again. Be calm, cold, detached. Don't let emotions get in the way of doing what needs to be done—or let them push you into doing more than is needed to accomplish your mission.

Yes, but when vengeance pushes you in the same direction as your professional standard? The more the priests Ayocan suffered, the better his mission would be accomplished. And the more they suffered, the more they would also pay for what they had done, and forced Blade to do. On that thought he became calm, lay down, and went to sleep.

CHAPTER 16

Natrila kept her part of the bargain as well as she could, and Blade kept his as well as he could. It was easy for him not to tell Isgon. It was less easy for him to meet Natrila's demands for lovemaking. Not impossible—Blade had never failed that way yet. He suspected that when he did, it would be wise to take him off missions into Dimension X. In each new dimension his life or at least his success seemed to depend at least once on satisfying a sex-hungry woman. But he also hoped that his virility would last much longer than his career as a traveler into Dimension X.

Natrila's newly awakened appetites were large, and her desire to get more and learn more was enormous. Blade was kept busy when she visited him. In return, she kept him fairly well posted on the doings inside the temple. Not as well as he had hoped, because Natrila did not move around much. Nor did her father tell her very much. And of course she could hardly ask anything of the other priests, even the most trustworthy ones. But Blade learned that Isgon was rapidly pushing his plans forward. The ranks of the Death-Vowed were swelling steadily. Messages flowed regularly back and forth among the various temple mounds in Gonsara. The ones outside Dafar would have an important job to do when the day came—that of creating spectacular diversions. And a small net of sympathizers in key places was being built up in Dafar itself. Were they really sympathizers, or merely men lusting after power and gold? Blade did not know, nor did he care at

131

this point. One who served the cult of Ayocan was an enemy.

Even without Natrila's information it would have been obvious that Isgon was getting impatient. The second set of Holy Warriors was now in training, which gave a total force of close to a hundred men. But Isgon was continuously after Blade to start the third and even fourth groups training. Visions of Holy Warriors obedient to his orders marching by the hundreds and thousands through Gonsara were beginning to dance in the priest's head. Blade found it increasingly hard to convince him that it would be several months at least before as many as a thousand Holy Warriors were fit to tackle King Thambral's troops.

Twenty days passed, during which time Natrila came to Blade's chamber seven times. On the twenty-first evening, she came for the eighth time. And this time she brought some startling and even alarming news.

"An Elder Brother is coming to this House all the way from the Supreme House in Tzakalan. It is said he is planning to inquire into the affairs of the servants of Ayocan here in Gonsara. It is also said he will bring seventy or more Holy Warriors of his own, the pick of those from the Supreme House.

This was a time for Blade to once more pretend to be a devoted and faithful servant of mighty Ayocan. "What can he hope to find in such an inquiry? We have done not the smallest thing to displease Ayocan. And why seventy Holy Warriors? Does he think to replace those we have trained here? Seventy Holy Warriors will not be enough to even seize Thambral's palace, let alone bring Ayocan to power in Gonsara."

Blade was more worried than he could afford to show. Did this sudden mission from Tzakalan mean that the cult of Ayocan was on his trail again? Or perhaps they were on Isgon's trail? Either meant trouble for Blade, but the second also meant trouble within the ranks of the cult. Blade could hardly think of a more appealing sight

132

than the Holy Warriors of two different factions of the cult fighting it out in the main temple mound in Gonsara. He knew that his own men would certainly fight any attempt to disarm them unless both he and Isgon ordered them to submit. And certainly Blade was never going to give that order.

Four days later at about dinner time, word came of the Elder Brother's arrival. Blade picked the fifty best fighters from his Holy Warriors and led them to the uppermost levels of the temple mound. He and Isgon did not want the new priest's Holy Warriors penetrating any deeper than necessary into the temple mound. If it came to a fight, the closer to the surface the better. And for Blade himself, the closer to the surface he was, the faster he could get out, if necessary.

Blade distributed the men around the chambers and corridors and squatted on his haunches to wait. Within a few minutes a rumble floated down the stairs from the surface above. The sound of voices and the clank of weapons reached Blade. A troop of forty-odd Holy Warriors filled the stairs and lined up on either side of the door. Although they were disguised as porters and other manual laborers, their bearing gave them away, as did the swords and axes now worn openly on their belts. Next came the sound of sandaled feet briskly descending the stairs. Finally a small figure in yellow-orange robes stepped into sight.

It was Pterin.

As Blade stepped forward to greet Pterin, he recognized the man. He stiffened and stopped so abruptly that he nearly lost his balance and sprawled forward on his face at Pterin's feet. But he managed to stay upright, staring at the priest, searching for any sign of recognition on the thin face.

For the moment, there was none. Instead Pterin turned to Isgon and glowered at him while another troop of Holy Warriors filed down the stairs. By the time they had all reached the bottom, the chamber was packed almost solid with warriors and priests. The only open space was a small circle around the two Elder Brothers. Blade also noticed that a solid mass of Pterin's Holy Warriors stood between him and the foot of the stairs.

Now Pterin stepped up to Isgon and said coldly, "A strange greeting, Isgon. Whence come these men in the garb of the Holy Warriors of mighty Ayocan? I thought King Thambral had forbidden you such."

Isgon's hands fluttered nervously. Pterin's manner and the threatening force of tough fighters he had brought with him had the other priest much on edge. "They are being trained for me, in secret, by this warrior." He pointed at Blade, and motioned him forward, into the open circle. Reluctantly, Blade stepped forward. Under the circumstances the last thing he wanted was to be singled out for Pterin's attention.

Pterin's eyes swung toward Blade again. Their eyes met and locked, Blade once more searching for the slightest sign that Pterin saw through his disguise. Once more, he did not find it. And once more he still did not drop his alertness.

Isgon was explaining how Blade had come into the service of Ayocan. "—and after he slew four of the Death-Vowed with his bare hands, I knew that he was a warrior we should not, could not, let escape us. Certainly not when he offered the promise of our being able to train our own Holy Warriors here in Gonsara, and—"

"Perhaps," said Pterin icily. "But you had no permission from the Supreme Brother to admit this man, who might be anyone." Blade stiffened.

"But when he can train Holy Warriors—"

"For which you also have no permission from the Supreme Brother! What seek you here, Isgon? A private army of your own? What the House of Ayocan shall do in Gonsara is decided by the Supreme Brother, my ambitious friend. Not by you."

Isgon threw Blade a glance, appealing to him to order the local Holy Warriors into action. Blade shook his head.

That was a bad idea at any time, and particularly now, with Pterin's forces united and obviously alert.

Blade's shaking his head drew Pterin's eyes back toward him. "And *who* is this man you have admitted to the House of Ayocan? What has he to recommend him, besides his ability to help you break the laws of the Brotherhood?"

"I have already told you that—"

"I care not if he converted ten thousand of King Thambral's subjects to the worship of mighty Ayocan! He has been admitted to a House of Ayocan without proper testing and rituals. And you even permit him to wear a beard. That is to fly in the face of Ayocan. And Ayocan shall not be displeased." Pterin turned to his Holy Warriors and jerked a thumb at Blade. "Seize him, bind him, and shave him. His beard at least shall no longer pollute this house. After that I—"

Pterin never finished the sentence. Blade's arm snapped up, and his spear point flashed in the lamplight. Then the arm snapped forward, and the spear plunged into Pterin's chest. The priest's head jerked up, and his eyes met Blade's. "It—you—" he gasped. Then he choked on the blood welling up in his throat, reeled, and fell backward onto the floor.

Isgon and both groups of Holy Warriors stood in amazed shock for a moment. It was as if the spear that had killed Pterin had paralyzed all of them. In that moment Blade moved.

His axe and sword sprang into his hands. Brandishing both, he charged the warriors blocking his path to the stairway. The first two did not even have time to draw their swords, nor did Blade bother to use his weapons on them. He ploughed into them like a charging bull, hurling the two smaller men aside by sheer physical impact, smashing them to the floor.

Four more warriors stood between him and the stairs. One of them broke and ran from the spectacle of Blade coming at him. Blade let that man go. He had enough to

135

do with the other three. His axe sang through the air and crunched into the first man's shoulder, disabling his sword arm. A kick to the same man's kneecap sent him to the floor, gasping with pain and obviously out of the fight.

But the other two had their swords out now. Blade had to ward off a down-cut from the one to the right as he swung his axe toward the left. The first man's sword clanged off Blade's guard, while at the same moment Blade's axe chopped into the second man's neck. The man's head did not fly off, but it lolled hideously. Blood spurted over Blade, and for a horrible moment he thought he was going to lose his grip on his sword.

But he held onto it, feinted at his last opponent's head, then swung over and down to slash into the warrior's thigh. It was not a killing wound. But the warrior reeled out of Blade's path, and the stairway was open. Bloody axe and bloody sword waving, Blade tore up the stairs, taking them two and three at a time.

He barely felt or saw the stone under his feet. It was a small miracle that he reached the top without falling. But he did, and before there were any sounds of pursuit from below. The whole battle had taken thirty seconds at most. The mass of stunned and amazed warriors below would only be recovering from the shock and getting ready to follow Blade.

Several of Blade's men were on guard duty in the hut at the top of the temple mound. They had their swords already drawn when he came tearing up the stairs, no doubt alerted by the uproar from below. They stared at Blade as he darted toward the door. One of them raised a spear. Another asked, "Master, what is—?" But before he could complete the question, the door slid open. Several of Pterin's disguised Holy Warriors ran in, swords also drawn.

But Blade was not caught by surprise. He shouted "Treason! Blasphemy!" over his shoulder. Then he grabbed one of the staring temple guards and shoved him hard into the path of the oncoming Holy Warriors. The wretched man screamed as three swords chopped into him. But his dying strength kept him on his feet, so that he plunged among the Holy Warriors. He and they went down with shouts and clatters of falling weapons and waving arms and legs. Blade leaped high, sailing clear over the tangle of bodies. He cut at an exposed head as he went, and landed outside in the cool darkness.

There were other Holy Warriors still on guard outside, but Blade caught these by surprise. Before they could recover from that surprise, Blade had chopped down the only one who stood in his path. Before the others could close around Blade, he was out on the slope of the mound. The moon rode high over Dafar, brightly illuminating the slope. The stone was dry, and the footing was good. Blade thrust his sword into its scabbard, hung his axe on his belt, and settled down to run.

As he hit his stride, Holy Warriors from inside the mound began pouring out. They were shouting and waving their arms. In the bright moonlight Blade could see blood on some of them. There had been a fight down below, that was obvious. But more and more Holy Warriors kept pouring out into the open. A few, braver or angrier than the rest, started down the mound after Blade. For the moment, he had a safe lead. But he went down the side of the slope at a dead run, the wind whistling in his ears and his feet thudding on the stone.

He looked back again when he reached ground level. The Holy Warriors were coming after him now as fast as they could run. One at least came down the mound too fast. Blade saw him stumble and go rolling down the stone, arms and legs flying doll-like. But some of the others were coming down just as fast and staying on their feet. And now Blade saw that some of his pursuers were carrying spears. He would have to keep a longer lead than he had expected. One lucky hit or even a bad graze could slow him down enough to finish him.

Where should he run? He wished now that he had spent

more time exploring Dafar before entering the temple mound. But at least there had been maps in the temple mound. He knew that he was less than a mile from the edge of the built-up area of Dafar, where it spread out into the open country beyond. He did not know that country, but neither would Pterin's goon squads. With reasonable luck he would also find the people on his side, and against his pursuers. He turned toward the east, toward the open countryside, and once more settled down to run.

As Blade and his pursuers raced up the moonlit streets, he was able to keep a good twenty yards between him and them without effort. He would have liked to widen the gap still more. Twenty yards was too easy a spearcast, even for men perhaps not used to the weapon. But for the moment there were more than twenty of the Holy Warriors tearing along after him, too many to risk fighting when they could see him coming and get ready to face him. When some of them started dropping out, however . . .

The chase continued in deadly silence. The Holy Warriors had no wish to arouse a hostile people from their sleep. And Blade had even less wish to involve innocent people in a fight with the Holy Warriors of Ayocan. But, on the other hand, if they met a troop of King Thambral's soldiers . . .

They met none, and the chase continued in lonely silence. Only the thud of feet on the dirty stones of the street and the heaving breathing of hard-running men broke that silence. Blade risked another look behind him. A few of the Holy Warriors had dropped out or back, but a good fifteen were still coming on hard. Pterin must indeed have picked the very best of all the Holy Warriors of Chiribu's temples to follow him on his mission.

What would happen to the Gonsaran temple mounds, now that Pterin was dead? In particular, what would happen to Isgon and Natrila for sheltering Blade? With Pterin dead, there might be no one of rank superior to Isgon. The Gonsaran Elder Brother would then once more be ruler in his own House. On the other hand, there might be another Elder Brother among Pterin's followers, ready to deal with Isgon and Natrila. How he would deal with them was not a pleasant thought.

But there was another equally unpleasant thought, one that Blade could not shake off. If Isgon survived and regained control of the Gonsaran temples, he would not be out of danger. Another Elder Brother could always descend on him, with an even larger force of disguised Holy Warriors and perhaps Death-Vowed. Isgon's only hope for survival would be to launch his Death-Vowed against the rulers of Gonsara as soon as he could. With Gonsara thrown into chaos by his efforts, he would have a strong card to play if any protests or threats came down on his head.

And if Isgon fell? Whoever succeeded him would have an equal need for a swift success. He would have to knit the shaken and divided Gonsaran temple mounds together again into a fighting unit. Such a man would be just as likely as Isgon to order out the Death-Vowed.

Blade had planned to flee into the country and remain there for a time. Within a week or two the hunt for him would die out, and he could safely return to Dafar and find means of passing what he had learned on to King Thambral. But now he would have no time. He would have to get to King Thambral as fast as possible and warn him.

All this ran through Blade's mind in a few seconds, without slowing down his pounding feet. Now he once more tried to recall the maps of Dafar. The High Palace of the Kings lay not far from the river, on the northern edge of the city. For the moment, Blade was running almost directly away from it. Could he turn about and cut back across Dafar toward the palace? Not without a fight with the dozen-odd men who were still on his trail.

As he looked back toward them, the moonlight sparked on a raised spearhead. Then the spear flashed through the air toward Blade. He cut sharply to the right. The spear sailed past him. Blade heard the *wsssh* it made cutting through the air and the *clank* its bronze point made on the stones. A moment later another spear sailed toward him, and again he had to shift sideways. Again the spear missed, but this time bits of stone gouged up by its point hit Blade in the leg. If he turned back toward the river, he would be giving his enemies a chance to cut him off, more than a chance to put at least one spear through him. And one would be enough.

But not far from the edge of the city the map had shown a second royal palace. The Summer Palace of the Queen, the map had called it. Blade remembered that, and he also remembered what King Hurakun had said about the current Queen of Gonsara. Young, Hurakun had told him, and susceptible to being influenced. A good person for Blade to start with, now that he had a tale to tell. Even if the queen herself were not at the Summer Palace, certainly he could find a sanctuary there, and an opportunity to quickly get word to King Thambral.

The Summer Palace was barely half a mile away, almost due south from where Blade was now. He would still have to turn and risk being cut off. He threw another look backward. There were still ten or eleven men after him, at least half a dozen of them with spears.

Blade took the first corner he came to at a dead run, swinging to the right without missing a step. The new street sloped upward slightly. Blade hoped that would slow his pursuers more than it would him. But he could not help realizing that his own breath was beginning to come short, his legs starting to ache, and his eyes to sting from the sweat pouring down into them.

His pursuers made the turn and flung themselves after him. One of them also flung a spear, and this time Blade felt the disturbed air of its passage on his skin. An inch closer, and the spear would have hit him. He forced his legs to move faster, and saw the gap between him and his pursuers open up a little. Not much, but enough so that the next two spearcasts came nowhere near him.

The slope was getting steeper now, and the houses on either side of the street were larger and more luxurious. Once Blade saw a head stuck out of a bronze-decorated gatehouse as he pounded past. Then the owner of the head saw Blade's pursuers, and hastily withdrew.

Still steeper, still higher, and now the branches of tall trees trailed over the street. Twigs and leaves flogged Blade's face as he ran, and he felt his eyes water and small cuts open on his skin. The blood ran freely out onto his sweat-slick cheeks and mixed with his perspiration. For a moment he had to slow down. The men behind him promptly gained several yards. Another spear whistled toward him. The trailing branches dragged it to a stop in midair and it clattered onto the stone well behind Blade. Then he was out from under the trees and in the open street again.

As the men behind him struggled through the trees, Blade caught sight of a high gray wall less than a hundred yards ahead, closing off the end of the street. Most of the stone was heavily overgrown with climbing vines. But on one clear patch Blade saw the red-ox badge of the ruling house of Gonsara. The sight put extra strength into his legs. He was halfway to the wall before the men behind him burst out from under the trees.

Another spear smacked into the stone behind him just as he reached the wall and leaped at the vines. For a sickening moment he felt them sag and tear under his weight. Was he going to be able to climb them after all? Then his hands gripped the heavier stalks, and he began pulling himself monkeylike up the wall.

Behind him the sound of pounding feet died, as his pursuers stopped. Blade turned, and saw that four of them still carried spears. He turned back and began to climb faster. As long as he was on the wall he was a slow-moving, all but helpless target.

But the wall was nearly thirty feet high. Long before Blade could reach the top the men behind began throwing their spears. He was halfway up when one smacked against the wall inches from his neck. And he was two-thirds of the way up when a second gashed his thigh. He bit back a gasp and continued climbing. A third spear sailed past him as he reached the top of the wall and rolled himself up onto the flat vine-grown stones there.

He looked quickly at the wound. By good luck it was only a shallow flesh wound, from which the blood oozed slowly. It would handicap him in a fight or a run, but it would not kill him. Then he looked down the inside of the wall—and swallowed.

At the foot of the wall a wide moat of scummy water lapped at the moss-grown stones. In the water Blade could see silvery dartings and leapings, and once a fish leaped entirely clear of the water. It was one of the tiny carnivores from the river. Even if he hadn't recognized it, he would have known what lurked in the water. The bare and bleached skeletons of animals—cats, dogs, goats —and men lay half-submerged in the shallow water along the inner side of the moat.

The moat was at least ten feet wide. And on the inner side was a thorny hedge, another ten feet wide and at least ten feet high. Blade looked down into the street again. The men were still there, and now they had been joined by half a dozen more. The newcomers all carried spears. Getting back down the outside of the wall was hopeless. He would be skewered like a butterfly on a pin before he was halfway down.

Climb down inside, then. No, jump. He would have to clear the moat—falling among the fish would be certain death. The thorns at least would not kill him. Blade rolled over toward the inner edge of the wall, keeping as flat against the stone as he could. Even so, the motion must have attracted attention from outside. Still another spear flashed past him, clearing the wall and the moat, falling into the hedge with a crackle of branches. Blade hoped that wouldn't alert sentries inside. All he needed was to be skewered by other spears as he tried to untangle himself from the hedge.

Now he was on the inner edge of the wall. He took a deep breath and rose to a crouch. Again the motion attracted attention, again a spear flew at him. This one laid open the back of his left hand, making him wince. His luck was about to run out. Another deep breath. He braced himself, gritting his teeth at the pain from his gashed thigh. Then arms and legs uncoiled in a single mighty snap of muscles, and he was flying through the air.

He was falling as he flew, and the black scummy waters of the moat were coming up at him fast. For a moment he felt a chill certainty that he was going to land in the water among the fish. Then the water was no longer under him, and it was the thorn bushes that were coming up fast. They came up very fast, and then they rose around him and he landed with a terrific crash of branches.

The springy branches sagged and bent under Blade's weight, and the thorns slashed and pricked at his skin. The impact of his landing carried him almost down to the ground, the thorns gashing his skin every inch of the way. He ended up spread-eagled in the bushes, so thoroughly tangled in the branches and the creepers that he could barely move.

As his head cleared, he realized that he was near the inner edge of the bushes. He realized that small insects were already beginning to whine around him, attracted by the blood and sweat on his skin. And he realized with another shock that a tall figure stood on the grass just inside the hedge. Eyes gleamed in its face, eyes fixed on him.

CHAPTER 17

Blade tried frantically to wriggle out of the bushes, ignoring the extra stabs he received from the thorns. But the branches and vines held him as tightly as the tentacles of an octopus. After a moment he relaxed. If the person standing there watching him wanted to put a spear through him, there wasn't much he was going to be able to do about it. His axe had been torn from his belt when he hit the bushes, and he could not get at his sword.

Blade had just realized that the onlooker was unarmed, when the person threw back his head and laughed merrily. No—*her* head. It was a full, rich woman's voice, no mistaking that. Blade had to admit that perhaps his predicament was amusing to somebody else, but not to him. He muttered a string of curses under his breath. Then he started all over again on his efforts to untangle himself from the thorny hedge.

This time he was able to get a hand on the hilt of his sword, draw it, and lay into the branches. He would have given a good deal for a steel machete, but even the cold-worked bronze sword was better than bare hands. Bit by bit the branches and vines fell away from around him. After what seemed like hours, he finally staggered out of the hedge. His head was swimming from fatigue and loss of blood, but he managed to retrieve his axe. Then he very nearly fell flat on his face at the woman's feet. She laughed again, the laughter fading off into a giggle. Blade looked down at himself, and realized that he was for all practical purposes naked from his sandals up. The thorn-studded branches had ripped his shorts to bloody rags. He felt like swearing again, but this time kept silent. He had the sensation that the woman was sizing him up, and that it would be wisest to submit quietly to her examination. He stood there in silence, trying to keep his face expressionless and his hand away from his sword. He tried with less success to ignore the insects that continued to swarm around him.

Finally the woman appeared to have completed her examination, and laughed again. "Who or what pursued you, my friend? You came leaping over the walls as though starving wolves were after you."

Blade was not sure how much he should tell this woman. She was obviously of high rank, to be wandering freely in the Queen's Summer Palace. There were a fair number among the ruling class in Gonsara sympathetic to the cult of Ayocan. On the other hand, there were many who hated it as thoroughly as the average Gonsaran. Which was this woman? He saw her gaze harden, as she saw him hesitating.

"Well?"

"I was fleeing from Holy Warriors of the cult of the bat-god Ayocan. In some way I had incurred the enmity of the cult."

The woman's eyes widened, and her jaw set hard. There was anger in her, but anger at what? Him or the cult? Blade found it hard not to hold his breath.

Then to his relief the woman herself let out an oath. "Damn them! Thambral swore he would never let Holy Warriors into Gonsara. They must have slipped them in secretly. Do you know how they came to have Holy Warriors to pursue you?"

"I can tell you, my lady," said Blade shortly. Relief that the woman was at least for the moment on his side made him abrupt. "But I would rather not do it here. It is a rather public place. The men who pursued me may still be outside, and they have spears. If—"

But he did not need to explain any more. The woman

145

nodded and pointed toward the looming bulk of the palace. "You will indeed tell me." Now her voice was that of one accustomed to being obeyed. "But you need not do it here." Without a further word she turned her back on Blade, ignoring his drawn sword, and strode away through the trees. She moved so fast that in his battered state he had to push himself to keep up with her. .

She led him to a door on the ground floor of the palace, a small but heavy brass-bound door half-screened by tall bushes and short trees. It opened on a narrow staircase with a ceiling so low that Blade had to bend his neck to keep from bumping his head on the plastered stone. At the top of the stairs another door opened into a small, dimly lit antechamber. Pointed archways led from it into several other rooms. The woman motioned to a carved chest with cushions on top of it that stood in one corner.

"Sit there my friend. I think you had best have your wounds treated before you speak further. I do not think a surgeon is needed, though. I will summon the servants."

Blade looked a question at her, and she shook her head. "They will neither learn anything nor tell anything. They are deaf mutes." She turned aside, and pulled a cord hanging by the door.

The maidservants must have been within sight of whatever indicator the cord had moved. They scurried in through the door within moments. The woman's hands flickered in a complex series of gestures; the maidservants bowed and vanished as silently as they had come. After a longer interval they were back with a bucket of hot scented water and armloads of clean cloths. Some of these they soaked in the water and then used to sponge Blade clear. Whatever made the water smell also made it sting more than usual. The smart and pain of Blade's thorn wounds and spear slashes began to fade as the maidservants worked them over with the wet cloths.

The rest of the cloths they tore into strips and tied

around the larger wounds, particularly the ones in Blade's thigh and hand. Then they vanished again, this time to return with a large silver jug and two jeweled cups. Both jug and cups were marked with the ox-sign of the royal house of Gonsara.

Blade sniffed at the fumes rising from the cups. The woman smiled at him again. She had sat watching the servant girls minister to him with an almost expressionless face. Almost. There were hints of curiosity in her expression, curiosity about more than Blade's tales of the cult of Ayocan.

"It will do you no harm," said the woman. "Indeed, it will do you much good. Do you think I would do you harm now, before you and I—had talked of the cult of Ayocan?" There was a slight hesitation in that last sentence, and Blade had a weary suspicion what that hesitation concealed. Another highborn woman who wanted to have her fling before discussing urgent business. He looked at the woman, unsmiling, and saw her own smile fade as she saw the expression on his face. "Do you doubt my word?" she said, and there was unmistakably an edge in her voice.

Being stubborn with this woman would obviously do no good. Blade shook his head, slowly and reluctantly, then picked up his cup and sipped from it. The woman also picked up her cup, but drained it in a series of long gulps. Then she leaned back in her chair, sighing contentedly and licking her red lips. But her eyes did not leave Blade's face. There was nothing for him to do but to drain his own cup also.

For a short time Blade's only sensation was one of relief that he did not promptly fall on the floor and writhe in agony as poison burned out his insides. But he was still not sure that drinking the cup had been the wisest thing to do. He kept his eyes fixed on the woman, watching for some signs of triumph or anticipation on her face.

Before he saw any such signs, he felt signs of something else in his own body. Unmistakably, though perhaps embarrassingly, he was developing an erection. Stark naked as he was, there was no way of concealing it. There must have been a powerful aphrodisiac in the hot wine. And the woman had drunk that same wine. Would she soon be feeling the same sensations that were now beginning to flood through Blade? Trying to ignore his own increasing arousal, he kept watching her closely.

As he looked at her, he realized that she was younger than he had believed at first. Perhaps unconsciously, he had associated her height—only a couple of inches shorter than himself—and her poise with middle age or more. But all the skin he could see was firm and unlined, even the telltale skin of the neck. There were only the faintest lines about the corners of the wide dark eyes, and not a single strand of hair that wasn't jet black. Small sapphire earrings sparkled on each of her ears, and a sapphire bracelet glittered on one wrist. Definitely this was a woman of high rank, to dress so, wear such jewels, and have such chambers within the palace.

As time passed, it became obvious that the woman was also becoming aroused from the aphrodisiac. Her breath was coming faster, and so deeply that Blade could hear it from halfway across the room. A pale pink tongue kept creeping out and moistening half-parted red lips. The wide, dark eyes did not leave Blade, but they did roam up and down his body. Occasionally those eyes lingered on Blade's massive erection. It was not painful, but neither did it show any signs of going down at all.

Then suddenly the woman stood up with a wriggle of her hips, and came toward Blade. With a single fluidly graceful motion, she knelt before him. Blade saw that her eyes were now almost glazed with a rutting passion.

With that expression on her face, Blade expected the woman to fling herself on him, to impale herself on his swollen organ. But she did not. Instead she bent her head forward on its slender neck, her red lips wrinkling in hungry anticipation. A quick dart of her head, and those lips closed around Blade's erection. They held it for a moment without moving, then began a slow, steady, rhythmic motion.

If this woman ranked high in Gonsara, she also ranked high among the experts at fellatio Blade had met. He discovered this soon enough. She would work away, building him steadily, with a deadly sureness, toward climax. And then, without a word or a motion from Blade, she would sense when he was approaching the final loss of control. In that moment her lips would cease their movements for a moment. Blade would feel the pulsing and the pressure within him fade. But only for a moment. Soon she would start again, and they would repeat the whole sequence.

How often they repeated it, Blade didn't know. After two or three times, it seem ludicrous to keep count. After four or five, it became impossible. The work of those moist, mobile red lips around his organ, added to the stimulus of the drug, had Blade half-mad. He kept his eyes on the woman with a grim intentness. It was as if his eyes could strip off the gold-embroidered bodice and the shimmering red pantaloons, the jeweled sandals and bracelets, and reveal what lay beneath. Blade had a vague impression that the curves concealed by the woman's clothing were more subtle than usual. But they were definitely there, definitely female. Blade did not really have much attention to spare for anything except those lips that were engulfing him.

In time they stopped. Blade had become so nearly addicted to them that in that moment he felt an almost anguished disappointment. But then the woman rose to her feet and placed both hands on the jeweled silver clasp of her pantaloons.

"Yes, my friend, you shall have what more you want. And you shall give me what more I want, what I want and need." There was a thin smile on her face, but her deep voice was deepened still further and shaken by barely controlled passion. In those moments when she had been

149

steadily piling up Blade's passion, she had also been building up her own.

Her fingers moved swiftly, and with a faint click the clasp of her pantaloons slipped open. They began to sag and slide, drifting down past her waist, revealing a broad-flat stomach. They kept on sliding, and the beginning of a gentle outward curve of hips came into view. Then the woman grinned and spread her legs apart, stopping the descent of the pantaloons. She must have been watching Blade's eyes, because her grin broadened.

"Indeed, my friend, such disappointment. You *are* ready." Her hands moved again, this time up to the clasp that fastened her embroidered bodice in place. With another *click* that clasp also gave, and the bodice sagged open. More gentle curves came into view, the upper slopes of the woman's firm breasts. But this time the clothing did not stop moving. Slowly the bodice slipped down. Then suddenly she shrugged her shoulders and it slipped off completely and fell to the floor. Small rock-hard breasts sprang free, with smaller dark nipples standing up, engorged and firmed, into small jutting points.

The sight was too much for Blade's last fragments of self-restraint. He took two quick steps forward, and his arms went around the woman. His hands met at the small of her back and swiftly moved down under the waistband of her pantaloons. He clasped the satiny but firm buttocks. Involuntarily the woman gasped and her hips wiggled and jerked. The pantaloons slid the rest of the way down to the floor, landing in a heap about her feet. Blade could not see the dark hair that he knew must be covering her pubic mound. But he could feel it curling around his own engorged phallus as he pulled the woman hard against him.

As he did so, she gave a little leap, and came down on Blade's rigidity. It slid easily up into her already soaking interior. Her head went back and her eyes rolled up as her mouth opened to let out a moan of delight. For a moment she moaned so loud that Blade thought she was

150

already reaching climax. The idea very nearly pushed him over the edge, and he almost groaned with the effort not to release then and there.

After a moment the strain faded once again, and it was no longer an effort to keep a steady rhythm inside the woman. She grew wetter and wetter as Blade stroked away, moaning at each thrust. He felt her weight grow heavier and heavier on him and against him. She was losing the ability to stand by herself as more and more of her became centered around Blade's massive maleness thrusting steadily up into her. Blade found her pushing down on him harder and harder, as though she could not bear to have him withdraw from her even the least bit.

Eventually, inevitably, she reached her first climax, and her body shook like a tree in a high wind. All her weight came on Blade, and they both nearly fell to the floor. Her mouth opened and became slack, and moans and whimperings like those of a dying animal came out of it.

Blade very nearly reached his own climax while the woman was in the middle of hers. The jerkings and twistings of her body, both inside and outside, managed to stimulate him still more. But the woman's climax faded away seconds before it triggered off Blade's.

As she became momentarily helpless, Blade summoned up his last bits of strength and lifted the woman up and carried her into the bedroom. For those seconds he was no longer inside her, and she whimpered at the unwelcome sensation. Then he swung her onto the bed and lowered her onto the light padding. She whimpered again. Before she could whimper a third time, he was atop her and back inside her, and his thrusts were coming in a mounting rhythm again.

This time Blade did not try to pace himself or hold back or wait for the woman. He was past self-restraint and past good bedroom manners. He was past anything except releasing the raw passion that was once again building up in him.

It built up quickly now, and the release also came

quickly. The woman's second spasm came with Blade's. For a very long moment there were only two maddened animals thrashing about on the bed, uttering animals' moans and cries, without the smallest piece of reason left between them.

The moment of release and madness passed for both of them. Blade mustered up enough strength to roll off the woman instead of sagging down on her and flattening her into the mattress. But that was the last strength he could muster up for quite a while. The frantic bout of sex on top of the fight, the run, and the leap across the moat had thoroughly drained him.

Eventually his fogged vision cleared and his breathing slowed to something like normal. He felt enough strength returning to raise himself on one elbow and look down at the woman sprawled on the bed beside him. Her mouth was still sagging open, but life and reason were returning to her eyes also. Finally her mouth closed, she raised a hand to push tangled and sweat-soaked hair back from her eyes. Then once again her face broke in that oddly appealing grin.

"Perhaps I should say, 'Well done,' as I often say to a warrior who has distinguished himself," she said. "But perhaps other words are needed for this. There are any number of warriors in Gonsara strong in other parts of their bodies. But your strength extends farther than theirs, into one place more than theirs. Yes, you deserve something special."

This seemed to require some comment from Blade. "Perhaps. But that is at your discretion—my lady."

"It is indeed at my discretion," said the woman with a grin. "I am Queen Jaskina of Gonsara."

CHAPTER 18

This remark also seemed to require some response from Blade. He could not very easily bow while lying on a bed. Nor could he quite see the need to be courtly and formal to the queen under the circumstances. He contented himself with a deferential nod and a murmured, "I am honored."

She patted him intimately. "As was I, my friend. And now perhaps you will tell me your name. We have not, after all, been properly introduced." The grin was back on her face as she said that.

Blade held yet another mental debate with himself over what to tell her. If she was telling the truth about being Queen of Gonsara, it was beyond possibility for her to be an ally of the cult of Ayocan. If she was lying—well, he would face that when and if he had to.

"I am a warrior from a distant people, the English. My name is Richard Blade. I did indeed make an enemy of the cult of Ayocan. But that was in Chiribu, where I came across the mountains from my part of the world into yours. Now I serve King Hurakun of Chiribu."

Without leaving out any of the crucial details, Blade told Jaskina of what he had done and what he was supposed to do. The queen listened in silence, her eyes fixed on Blade's face, and her lips drawn tight over her even white teeth. All during Blade's tale there was not the slightest trace of the ready grin on her face. And she only spoke once, after Blade mentioned killing Pterin.

"I wonder—do you think he knew who was killing him?"

"I have wondered about that myself. I rather doubt it."

"That is too bad. It would have made his death just that much harder. And the priests of Ayocan one and all deserve a hard death. Now perhaps we can see that they get it."

"We?"

"You and I. At last King Thambral will have to believe that the cult of Ayocan is a deadly danger."

"I did not think he was ignoring it before, your Majesty."

"No, but he wished to be just and legal about dealing with it. And he wished above all things peace with Chiribu."

"A good wish, I should think." Blade had a vague and disagreeable feeling that hidden meanings were lurking in Jaskina's words. He wanted to draw more out of her.

"No doubt, under most circumstances. But peace with Chiribu, at the cost of ignoring such a deadly threat? That is not wise. And now the threat extends to the very existence of the Throne of the Red Ox." Again Blade had the impression of hidden meanings.

And again he decided to test Jaskina. "Indeed it does. I don't know when the Death-Vowed will be turned loose against you and Thambral and perhaps others among the highly placed of Gonsara. But I suspect it will be soon. Certainly within a few days, perhaps even tonight. I think—"

"Indeed, it might very well be tonight," said Jaskina slowly. "Well, my own household is well protected, as you know." She pointed at Blade's thorn wounds. "Once the gate guards are alerted, not even the Death-Vowed will be able to get in. And if they do, I have you, as a second line of defense."

"Your Majesty, I must go to the palace of King Thambral and warn him also. Otherwise his guards may not be alert, and the Death-Vowed may break through them and kill him."

"Yes, they might." The total calm in Jaskina's voice as she said that bothered Blade. "Indeed, they might. But—"

"Yes, your Majesty. *But*—" There was an edge in Blade's voice now, as suspicions grew in him.

"But I think if Thambral will not take proper precautions by himself, is there any reason to help him? The gods take small care for fools, so why should we do more than they?"

There were any number of possible answers to that question, but Blade gave none of them. Suspicion had become certainty. If Queen Jaskina was not on the side of the cult of Ayocan, she certainly had ambitions of her own. And she was as ready as any Elder Brother of the cult to see King Thambral's life spurt out under the swords and axes of the Death-Vowed.

This definitely was a surprise for Blade, and a thoroughly unpleasant one. It was what J would have called "a most infernally disagreeable complication." Between one minute and the next, Jaskina had gone from probable ally to almost certain enemy. She was looking hard at him now, and Blade had to avoid meeting her eyes. If he had done so, she would have seen his new knowledge and his new hostility there as clearly as if they had been written on the wall in letters a foot high.

As it was, she did not see it and react to it until Blade had rolled out of bed and put a safe distance between himself and the queen. That was just as well. When Jaskina did realize what Blade was thinking, she screamed like a panther in its death agony. Then she rolled out of bed and dashed for the cord to summon the servants.

Fortunately the pillows on the bed were large and heavy. Blade snatched one up and flung it across the room after Jaskina, aiming low and hitting her in the back of the legs. She staggered, stumbled, and went down. Blade leaped over the bed, pain from his wounded leg

155

stabbing through him. He reached Jaskina and fell on top of her just as she was reaching for the pull-cord.

She screamed again as he landed on her, and then all her breath went out of her in a whoosh. She went almost completely limp, but Blade did not let go of her. He didn't trust her out of his sight or out of his hands, and he began looking around the room for something to use to tie her up. Then he would have to get out of the palace as fast as possible. He had just decided on using the sheets from the bed when he heard the sound of several sets of running feet outside the door. Along with the feet he heard heavy breathing, and then two shrill screams. One was a woman, obviously not a mute, dying in agony and terror. The other was unmistakably the scream of one of Ayocan's Death-Vowed.

As the woman's scream died away in a choking gurgle, Blade leaped to his feet and darted for the door. Jaskina also leaped to her feet and ran in the opposite direction, toward the inner chambers of her apartment. Blade didn't worry about her. For the moment he could only afford to worry about getting out of this palace, through a swarm of Death-Vowed. And they would doubtless make him their main target the moment he stuck his nose out into the corridor.

If he hadn't been able to lay hands on his sword and axe, his situation would have been desperate. But he found both and snatched them up just as the door gave inward, with a splintering of wood and a *spang* of metal hinges coming apart. Three of the Death-Vowed charged through the open doorway, eyes wide in frenzy and mouths open.

They were too blind with fury and the drug that was in them to notice Blade until he leaped at them. The first one he struck died in mid-scream. The scream was cut off abruptly as Blade's axe smashed through the man's ribs and tore apart everything behind them. Then the scream became a gurgle as blood welled up in the man's throat and spurted out of his mouth. The man's terrible drug-

156

given vitality kept him on his feet and moving forward. But he was now only a blinded, maimed animal, blundering forward until he collided with the wall and fell to the rug.

The death of the first Death-Vowed alerted the other two. But they were blindly, madly determined to have Blade's death, so they did not retreat. At least not far enough to escape him. His sword whistled low and took one in the thigh. His axe struck overhand and came down on a shoulder, shearing through flesh and bone. Neither blow killed, but both crippled. This time the two Death-Vowed did draw back, enough for Blade to charge between them and out into the corridor.

Now the two Death-Vowed ignored Blade, and lurched forward into the queen's chambers. Would they have enough strength left to find Jaskina and strike her down? For a moment Blade considered going back to finish them off and save the queen. It went against his grain to leave any woman to be slaughtered like a pig by the Death-Vowed of Ayocan.

That moment of doubt was enough for three more of the Death-Vowed to come charging down the hall. In front of them ran one of the deaf-mute servant girls, her mouth open in what should have been a scream of terror. It stayed open in agony as the Death-Vowed caught her and sank their axes into her skull, shoulders, and back. Blood spurted from her mouth as she fell forward and writhed on the carpet. The axes sank into her back again, and she lay still.

Before the Death-Vowed could free their axes and rise to meet Blade, his own weapons came down at them. His sword sliced through the back of a neck, a ragged and imperfect cut that left the head dangling. But not even a Death-Vowed's unnatural vitality could keep the man on his feet after that wound. He fell onto the body of his victim, and lay still.

Before the first Death-Vowed struck the floor, Blade's axe smashed into the forehead of the second. But his bandaged left hand could not grip the axe properly, and it turned in his hand as he struck. Only the flat of the head struck the Death-Vowed, and that only half-stunned him. He took a lurching step forward, and his sword came down with a clang on Blade's, so hard that the shock ran up Blade's arm and jarred his whole body.

Blade backed away, feinted at the man's head again with his axe, and then slashed sideways at the man's stomach. The Death-Vowed was moving forward at that moment, and the tip and a good six inches of bronze sank into his stomach. In the next moment the third Death-Vowed leaped at Blade, striking with both sword and axe. Blade blocked the axe with his own. But his sword was just pulling free of his second victim's stomach. The third Death-Vowed's sword came down on Blade's with a terrible crash. This time the shock was so great that even Blade's unwounded right hand could not keep its grip on his sword. The sword fell to the rug. The Death-Vowed closed again. He screamed in triumph as well as rage when he saw that he now had two weapons against a man armed with only one.

Blade saved himself by another tremendous leap. It opened a gap six feet wide between him and the last Death-Vowed. For a moment the two men—the one that was still human and the one whose humanity had been sucked out of him by the cult of Ayocan—stood staring at each other.

In that moment another scream, more ghastly than anything that had come before, echoed down the hall. Unmistakably it was a woman's voice. And it was coming from Queen Jaskina's chambers. The two Death-Vowed Blade had maimed but not killed had indeed found her. Now all her plans and schemes were dying under their bronze swords and stone axes.

Blade would not have regretted that too much even if he had been able to spare the time and thought for the dying queen. The scream was still hanging in the air when several things happened almost at once. The third

158

Death-Vowed charged at Blade, waving both sword and axe, screaming in a voice that drowned out Jaskina's death rattle. Blade leaped aside from the man's rush and set his back against the wall, raising his axe.

As he did so, screams and pounding footsteps sounded from his right. Two more Death-Vowed burst out of the stairway there. But they reeled and lurched as they ran, and the chest of one and the back of the other were pumping blood. They charged blindly past Blade and straight into their advancing comrade. They struck just as blindly at him as they would have at Blade. And their comrade was too surprised to defend himself. He died with his eyes widening in amazement and his mouth widening in a scream of terror.

Somehow the realization that they had slain one of their own penetrated the minds of the two surviving Death-Vowed. They stood motionless, eyes wide and staring down at the body slumping to the rug at their feet. Before they could move to meet the new threat, Blade struck. His axe chopped deeply into one man's thighbone, then rose in a whistling arc to slice cleanly through a neck. The severed head soared into the air, then dropped to the rug with a thump and rolled over and over toward the head of the stairs.

It stopped rolling almost at the feet of two gigantic men in the pantaloons and sashes of Gonsaran soldiers. They popped out of the stairway like genies from bottles. Then they stopped with blood-smeared swords in their hands, and stared down the corridor. Their eyes took in the blood on the rugs and walls, the sprawled bodies, and Blade leaning against the wall. Their swords came up as their eyes fell on him. And he straightened and raised his axe as he felt their gaze on him.

"Who in the name of the eighty-one spirits of death are you?" snapped the smaller of the two soldiers.

Blade took a deep breath. "A warrior of the English."

"Who in the name of—?" began the same warrior, but his comrade stopped him.

"Have you been fighting the Death-Vowed of Ayocan?" said the second warrior.

Blade was too weary to be polite. "What does it look like?"

The warrior grinned briefly. "I see. Well, the fighting is over for the moment. I think—"

It was Blade's turn to interrupt. "I think you had best see to Queen Jaskina. I saw two of the Death-Vowed enter her chambers, and heard screams. And I also think you would do well to take me to King Thambral. I have much to say to him that concerns the safety of Gonsara, and I would prefer to save it for his ears alone."

How Blade managed to scrape up enough strength to speak in that commanding tone, he never knew. But it did the job. Accustomed from long training to obey any order snapped out in the appropriate tone of voice, the two soldiers bowed their heads. Then the first one turned and shouted down the stairs.

"Come up, come up, comrades. The Death-Vowed are slain, and a man here seeks audience with King Thambral."

CHAPTER 19

It took the Gonsarans several days to sort out all the pieces and count the bodies. And they had more important things to do than keep Blade informed about the proceedings. So Blade spent those several days in "protective custody" in the basement of the Summer Palace. He wasn't sure if the Gonsarans were more interested in the "protection" or the "custody." But his cell was dry, warm, and well furnished, and the food and drink were both good and abundant. So he assumed he was in reasonably good standing with the Gonsaran authorities. At least he was not suspected of sympathy with the cult of Ayocan. Whether he was suspected of having had something to do with Queen Jaskina's death, he wasn't sure. Apparently nobody gave much thought to the late queen. Considering what she had been planning or at least hoping for, neither did Blade.

But bits and pieces of information did trickle into Blade's gilded cage. Out of those bits and pieces Blade put together a fairly good picture of what had happened the night of Jaskina's death and for a day and a night afterward.

When the uproar in the temple mound caused by Pterin's death was over, Isgon had indeed regained command. And Blade's guess had been right. The priest saw that throwing Gonsara into chaos was his best chance of survival. So the Death-Vowed had gone out, more than three hundred of them in one massive and desperate attack.

161

But they had not fallen upon unwarned or unprepared victims. The man in the gatehouse who had watched Blade and his pursuers rush past had sent the word to his master. His master, one of Thambral's principal generals, had alerted his own troops and also sent word to the High Palace.

The defense could not be perfect, nor was it. Jaskina's guards and servants had been overpowered and some forty of them besides the queen herself slaughtered. One of the royal princes had also died, with his wife and two of their children and various guards and servants. But Thambral had four other sons and five daughters. There had also been casualties among the high military and civilian functionaries.

King Thambral himself spent that night in the Refuge Chamber of the High Palace. It had been built for just such disorderly occasions, and it served the House of the Red Ox well. To get to Thambral, the Death-Vowed would have had to slay every fighting man in the palace and then break through twenty feet of solid stone. They did not even do the first, although every one of them died trying.

Much the same happened to the Death-Vowed elsewhere. When dawn rose over Dafar, almost the entire three hundred lay dead in their blood in palaces and streets and gardens. And then King Thambral emerged from the Refuge Chamber, addressed his soldiers from the balcony of the High Palace, and sent them out to destroy the cult of Ayocan in his kingdom.

This they did. The priests died to the last man, from Isgon down to the newest Brother with the ink barely dry on his vows. So did the Holy Warriors, who fought back with a courage and skill that was a credit to Blade's training, if not to their own judgment. Strict orders spared the slaves and eunuchs and temple prostitutes. The soldiers merely rounded these up and confined them while the killing of the priests and Holy Warriors went on to its end. By the evening of the second day there was not a known Brother or Holy Warrior of Ayocan alive in Dafar. And troops of cavalry were pounding out of the capital in all directions, to purge and cleanse the other cities of Gonsara in the same way.

On the morning of the fourth day, Blade was called before King Thambral. By then, the only thing he did not know that preyed on his mind was the fate of Natrila. It would be a hard fate for the poor girl, to be swept away with her father in the general slaughter of all who were thought to serve Ayocan.

King Thambral met Blade in his private Hall of Audience, hung with trophies of arms and wild beasts taken or slain in the king's younger days. Those were far behind now. The years had thinned him down to almost skeletal leanness, and whitened his hair. He looked as though a strong wind might carry him away into the sky. But his eyes were clear and intense, and his voice low but clear as he interrogated Blade.

Blade held back nothing about his mission in Gonsara nor about what he had done the night of the cult's attack. He felt he could trust the old king to judge wisely. But he still had tense moments when he finished his story and stood with Thambral gazing silently at him.

Then Thambral's wrinkled lips creased in a brief smile. "Well, Richard Blade. That is a considerable story you have told me."

"It is only the truth, your Majesty."

"I know that," said Thambral testily. "I am not doubting your word. You appear honest, and much of what you have said I have also heard from others. But it is still most impressively full of adventures survived and perils escaped. Your wits seem to work as fast as your sword."

"I hope so, your Majesty."

"So do I. You are not through with your service to the House of the Red Ox. You will give me good service for some time yet, whether King Hurakun says yea or nay. Otherwise . . ." Thambral brought his hands together and made a neck-twisting gesture. Blade nodded.

163

Thambral went on. "I do not see King Hurakun saying nay, though. You need only help with the final destruction of the cult of Ayocan. When they are gone from the earth, you may return to Hurakun's service. You may even return to your own people, for all that I care."

Blade was surprised by the fierceness in Thambral's voice as he spoke of the cult. The surprise must have shown on his face. Thambral smiled again and said, "You wonder that I speak so against the Ayocani? I did not, once. I wanted to live at peace for the few years remaining to me, at peace even with the Ayocani. But peace is something that both must seek for both to have it. The cult certainly seeks no peace. And therefore they shall not have it."

He sighed. "I grieve somewhat that you slew that Elder Brother, Pterin. He would have been most informative about the plans of the cult, I imagine. Of course he would doubtless have had to have been encouraged a trifle before he spoke. But I have those in my service who can encourage a stone statue to speak if they are given enough time."

Blade shrugged. "At the time I could hardly spare him, your Majesty. I needed his silence, not his speech."

"To be sure," said Thambral. "I am not going to pass judgment on you. We will have enough to lay before Hurakun to persuade him as it is."

"And if he is difficult to persuade?" Blade ventured. "The cult has enough true members in Chiribu to somewhat tie Hurakun's hands."

"Somewhat, indeed," said Thambral. "But he had best untie his own hands, or face war with Gonsara. Yes, I know that could play directly into the hands of the Ayocani. But there are none of those left in Gonsara. None to rule it or even to strike at it from the rear. And as for Hurakun—" Thambral shrugged. "You know him as well as I do. Would you say he would really *rejoice* in fighting Gonsara to aid only the Ayocani?"

Blade had to laugh at the idea. "Hardly, your Majesty.

He would march to such a war with all the eagerness of a boy on his way to school. And he would be glad of any reasonable excuse not to march at all."

Thambral smiled. "I thought as much. Then we shall give him such an excuse. The orders to mobilize my army have already gone out, and likewise the orders to my River Fleet. We shall put one army marching over land, and another aboard the fleet to sail up the river. Thus we can carry war into the very heart of Chiribu if we choose. But I do not think we will have to do so. Tell me, Blade. How many of Hurakun's subjects are so devoted to Ayocan that they will see their homes and crops burned and their families slaughtered to avenge the offended honor of the bat-god?"

Blade's face gave his answer. "Exactly," went on Thambral. "Hurakun can say to his people, 'Is it truly your wish that I lead you by the tens of thousands to your deaths in battle merely for the sake of Ayocan?' I wonder how many of them will say yes?"

Blade had to laugh out loud. "Your Majesty, I am beginning to think King Hurakun had no need to send me to your lands. The true gods know the Ayocani had no need for another enemy in Gonsara. Not with you sitting on the throne."

Thambral laughed also. "For that compliment you deserve some reward above what I was already planning to give you."

"Your Majesty?"

Thambral made no reply, but instead rang a bell. A servant ran in and prostrated himself before Thambral. The king murmured a few words, inaudible to Blade, into the man's ear, and dismissed him.

The servant was back within a few minutes. Behind him were four soldiers carrying a curtained litter. Thambral smiled at the bewilderment on Blade's face. "Go on, Blade. Open the king's gift." Blade stepped up to the litter, jerked open the curtain—and Natrila wriggled out and into his arms.

When he had untangled himself from her and could turn to face the king, Thambral was grinning still more broadly. "She should not have said that she was Isgon's daughter. When she said that, my soldiers very nearly slew her on the spot. But when she mentioned your name, she was saved." Thambral stood up and made a gesture of dismissal. Blade bowed and started to lead Natrila out of the chamber.

He was just passing out the door when Thambral called after him, "Don't use up all your strength on her, Blade. Save some of it for the march north. We will be on our way within a week, perhaps two at the most. And you will be with me."

CHAPTER 20

Twenty thousand of Thambral's soldiers were on the march north from Dafar within a week. Meanwhile ships and barges and war galleys came into the docks of Dafar from all along the river. Five thousand armed soldiers and ten thousand more soldiers climbed aboard them, and two weeks later they sailed north. Toward the middle of the third week, a messenger came to Blade in the gray dawn as he lay beside Natrila. Before she had drifted off to sleep, she had said she was carrying his child.

"Warrior Blade, King Thambral commands you."

"How?"

"That you be aboard his flagship at noon today. He sails to join his fleet and army on the borders of Gonsara."

"I will be there."

It cost him more pain than he had expected, to say goodbye to Natrila. She was as worried about him as if he had been going into a full-scale war. And he also knew that it was long odds against his being able to return to her. He had been in this dimension a good while now. Sooner or later Lord Leighton's computer would reach out across the dimensions and grasp his brain, plucking him home like a ripe fruit from a branch.

But after all the goodbyes, he was aboard Thambral's flagship when it sailed that noon. And he was on board it ten days later when it caught up with the rest of the Gonsaran forces. The fleet almost blocked the river, and the tents and horse-lines of the soldiers covered the land for a mile along either bank. The clear sky was hazed gray with smoke from the campfires on the land and the cookfires in the brick furnaces aboard the hundreds of ships.

Thambral's plan had worked—so far. The Gonsarans outnumbered the Chiribuan forces on the spot five or six to one. More important, the Chiribuans freely admitted they had orders to avoid a fight at almost all costs. If the Gonsarans did not cross the frontier, there would be no fighting.

The Gonsarans were more than willing to sit where they were, and so there was no fighting. But there was a constant exchange of messages between the two kings. Toward the end of the second week of the staring contest, a message arrived from King Hurakun. King Thambral promptly called Blade to his cabin.

"King Hurakun suggests that he and I meet on a barge in mid-river, to come to an agreement for dealing with the cult of Ayocan. He says he is willing to move forcibly against them as long as I keep my army and fleet on his borders. The danger from Gonsara, he says, has most people unwilling to fight or die for the cult. In fact, he says his army and fleet would quite possibly mutiny if he asked them to fight." Thambral leaned back in his chair and cracked his knuckles. "You have heard Hurakun in person on this matter more recently than I. What do you say? Can I trust him?"

"I think Hurakun is telling the truth. You can trust him, at least."

Thambral nodded. "I see. Do you think there is someone I cannot trust, among the House of the Serpent?"

"Yes. Second Prince Piralu. I have never met him, unfortunately, so I can only tell you what I have heard." Blade summarized his knowledge of the Second Prince. Thambral's lean face grew sober.

"I see," he said again. "You think Piralu may make this meeting an occasion for treachery?"

"Yes, and the crudest sort of treachery. Consider, your Majesty. The kings of both Gonsara and Chiribu will be together in a single ship in the middle of the river. If a

168

boatload of Holy Warriors and Death-Vowed were to slip alongside . . ."

Thambral frowned. "You think Piralu is that desperate?"

"By now—yes, your Majesty. Without the cult of Ayocan he will have small hope of grasping power. The Holy Warriors were to have been *his* army as well as the Supreme Brother's. Now, though, he can see the end of the cult approaching. I can only say that if I were in his position, I would certainly make one final effort."

"That may be true, Blade. But I can hardly bring wargalleys to the meeting. Hurakun specifically asks that I come to the barge with only one ship."

"That need not be a problem, your Majesty. The ship will have to have a crew and rowers, will it not? Why not have both the crew and the rowers alike be picked warriors of your household? A loincloth and a little dirt will disguise a man quite well. And their weapons could be hidden under the rowing benches or such places."

Thambral laughed. "Indeed, Blade, I think you would be a more proper servant for King Hurakun than for myself. Your mind works not unlike that of the serpent that is the badge of his house. It shall be done as you suggest. And I hope you will keep your weapons close at hand also. I do not imagine that you would care to miss the chance of dealing with a few more of Ayocan's servants."

"No, your Majesty. I would not."

So Blade was fully armed two days later as he stood on the foredeck of Thambral's royal yacht, watching the conference barge creep closer across the water. Hurakun's black-painted galley was already moored to the other side of the barge, and Blade could see black-clad figures moving about on its deck. As the Gonsaran yacht crept closer, Blade recognized Hurakun, Kenas, and Mirasa aboard the galley. But where was Piralu? Blade raised his eyes from the barge to where the fleet of Chiribu lay anchored in a long line across the river. He tried to make out the flags on the anchored warships and troop barges, but the sun was too nearly in his eyes.

The Gonsaran yacht scraped alongside the barge. The disguised warriors that made up its crew leaped onto the barge's deck with mooring lines. Some of them stumbled and nearly fell, for they lacked the normal surefootedness of sailors. Nobody in the Chiribu delegation seemed to notice or care, though.

Blade wore his weapons openly and undisguised as he helped the crew lay the gangplank across the railing of the Gonsaran yacht. As its end dropped with a thud onto the deck of the barge, Blade turned his eyes to the north again. Sunlight still danced blindingly on the water, but Blade thought he saw a black-plumed figure climbing down the side of a troop barge into a small boat. He blinked, and looked again. The small boat scurried out of sight behind a large war galley. Blade turned back to matters more at hand. He drew his sword and prepared to help King Thambral across the gangplank.

The musicians aft blew a fanfare on their coiled brass trumpets. Like the "sailors," the "musicians" today were not slaves or servants, but picked warriors of Thambral's household. And the "musicians," unfortunately, had not been picked for their musical ability. The fanfare sounded like an entire barnyard full of animals dying in agony. Blade cringed and shuddered at the noise. If he had not needed to maintain some ceremonial dignity, he would have clapped his hands over his ears.

The last of the barnyard finally died in peace, and the drummers took up the accompaniment. They were nearly as ragged, if less agonizing to listen to. Then King Thambral strode out on deck. His robes of state were brilliant green silk, so heavily encrusted with jewels and gold embroidery that Blade could hardly see the underlying color. What the robes might weigh Blade did not even want to imagine. But Thambral strode forward, as erect as if he had been wearing garments made of spiderwebs. He nodded to Blade, then stepped up to the gangplank and raised a hand in salute to Hurakun. Hurakun returned the salute. Thambral nodded to two of the disguised warriors, and they lifted him onto the gangplank. He took two slow steps forward. Blade turned, to look north again.

And this time he stopped in mid-turn. The big war galley he had noticed earlier was moving slowly out of its place in the Chiribuan line. As it did so, a gap of blue water showed. Through that gap were coming two low-slung boats, sails drum-tight with the north wind and oars pounding in a frantic beat. Both were black, the color of the House of the Serpent. But Blade recognized the type. They were the same as the temple boat that had launched the attack on the Lugsa.

For a moment Blade froze, then he spun completely around and began snapping orders. "Everybody—arm at once! Be ready to cut the lines and pull clear of the barge." His tone of voice made any argument impossible. The musicians and sailors scurried to obey. Then Blade turned to shout to King Thambral, who stood in the middle of the gangplank, staring about him at the sudden uproar.

As Blade turned, several things happened in rapid succession. Prince Kenas noticed the sudden activity aboard the Gonsaran yacht and shouted, "Treachery! They have —" Princess Mirasa noticed the oncoming boats, and screamed, "Treachery! Piralu has—" Before either prince or princess could finish, there was a whistle and a rushing in the air. Then there was a splintering crash as a solid chunk of rock crashed down on the barge's deck.

It landed squarely on one of Hurakun's counselors, smashing him to the deck, a pulped and bloody mess. Then it bounced off the deck, rolled, and crashed into the railing of the barge just to the right of where King Hurakun was standing. The railing splintered. The king, who was holding on to it, staggered. Then his massive black ceremonial headdress overbalanced him, and he plunged head-first over the side. His heavy black robes of state dragged him down out of sight even before the fish could gather around him to tear the flesh from his bones.

Prince Kenas uttered a great cry, "Father!" Princess Mirasa screamed wordlessly, madly, her clear wits and poise gone for the moment. King Thambral froze in the middle of the gangplank, and all the warriors seemed paralyzed with surprise. Then a second stone crashed down on the barge, and the gangplank lurched and threatened to spill Thambral into the river after Hurakun.

The only person not paralyzed was Blade. He sailed up onto the gangplank as though he were on springs. Dropping his sword, he seized King Thambral around the waist, lifted him high, and threw him bodily back aboard the Gonsaran vessel. Two of the warriors aboard the yacht snapped out of the paralysis in time to cushion their king's fall. Then as he felt the gangplank twist again and start to fall, Blade leaped, sprawling down with a crash on the deck of the barge.

He was on his feet again in a moment. "Quickly, your Majesty!" he shouted at Kenas. "Get aboard the Gonsaran boat. Now!" Kenas nodded. The realization that he was now king seemed to be filling him with new strength. He sprang up onto the railing of the barge, and without a moment's hesitation or teetering leaped high across the water. Mirasa screamed again. Then Kenas crashed down on the deck of the Gonsaran yacht, making the planks groan and flattening half a dozen Gonsaran soldiers like bowling pins. Before Mirasa could scream once more, Blade had snatched her up like a doll and flung her after her husband. He plucked her out of the air.

Now Blade shouted across the water to the crew of the Gonsaran yacht. "Get Kenas and Mirasa out of here. Back water and get out of here. Now!" He saw nods among the warriors, and heard rattles and bangs from below as the rowers ran out the oars. Water began to foam white around the yacht's stern as the rowers began to back her away from the barge. Now Blade felt that he could turn to meet the enemy.

The two cult boats were less than fifty yards away now, and coming on without slowing. On their bows he could

172

make out the frames of the two catapults that had hurled the stones. Their decks were crowded with armed men. As Blade watched, some of these pulled on the white bat-masks of the Death-Vowed of Ayocan. Blade ran quickly across the now deserted deck of the barge. He scrambled aboard the Chiribuan galley just as it too backed water and pulled clear of the barge.

He leaped down among the black-clad Chiribuan warriors just as another stone dropped between the barge and the yacht. Water splashed down on the yacht's deck. Blade saw some of the warriors cringe. He sprang onto the yacht's quarterdeck and shouted, "Hold there, warriors of Chiribu! Are you going to let King Hurakun die unavenged? It is in your hands. And remember—those who serve Ayocan are only men! They can die like men, whether it pleases Ayocan or not! And we shall see that they do die!" The warriors straightened and began to shout and cheer. Then the cheers and shouts were drowned out by a tremendous crash as the first of the temple boats rammed the galley in the stern. The howls of the Death-Vowed rose from the temple boat's deck.

But to get aboard the galley they had to pass over its quarterdeck, and to pass over the quarterdeck they had to pass Blade. They found this hard to do. The Death-Vowed swarmed and leaped in a blind frenzy. Some of them fell into the river. Blade stood his ground, took his time, and picked his victims out of the swarm with almost surgical precision. His axe and sword whistled and struck. More bodies living and dead fell down into the river. The water about the galley's stern boiled white and red.

Blade's whirling sword and axe held off the Death-Vowed for only a minute or so. But that was long enough for other warriors aboard the yacht to rally and join him. Together they met the rush of Holy Warriors swarming aboard to join the Death-Vowed. A savage battle with no holds barred and no quarter given or asked churned back and forth along the deck of the yacht. The smell of blood

173

and sweat, the clang of axes and sword, hideous screams from a dozen different throats rose thickly about Blade.

There was a brief moment when the fighting ebbed away from him and he was able to look beyond the galley's deck. The Gonsaran yacht was thrashing toward its own fleet line, with the other temple boat hard after it. The temple boat's deck was crowded with bat-masks. On the stern of the yacht Blade could see Prince—now King—Kenas standing tall, cursing and bellowing at the Ayocani. Several small galleys were slipping out of the Gonsaran line, toward the fleeing yacht, to cover its retreat.

He did not see whether they reached it before the temple boat. The Chiribuan warriors had to give way before a new rush of Holy Warriors. Blade had to shout and bellow and lay about him once again to rally them. He was completely lost in the battle frenzy that swept through him, smashing down with his axe, slashing with his sword, roaring and shouting with breath that came from somewhere. It was not until there were no more opponents around him that the frenzy ebbed. Once more he raised a head streaming sweat and blood to look around him.

Toward the Gonsaran fleet lay a tangled mass of boats, with the temple boat barely visible in the middle. A continuous rumble of battle rose from their decks, and swords and bat-masks flashed in the sun. Well beyond the tangle, the Gonsaran yacht was rowing sedately toward the shelter of the Gonsaran fleet. Straining his eyes, Blade could make out the figure of Kenas still decorating the yacht's stern.

Now the Chiribuan galley's decks were clear of Holy Warriors and Death-Vowed—at least of live ones. As Blade watched, the temple boat's oars thrashed, and it began backing away.

It did not get far. Two light Chiribuan galleys came down on it like hawks on a chicken. Short-handed as it had become, it did not last long against them. Within a few minutes one of the galleys pulled alongside Blade's.

174

Blade snapped at the first warrior to climb aboard from the galley. "Where is Prince Piralu?"

"His galley has gone upriver, sir. The Fleet Master has ordered out galleys in pursuit."

"Good. I want to be aboard one of them."

"Sir, I——"

"I said I want to be aboard one of them, my friend. Don't argue." Blade's voice was soft but deadly. That and his wild, blood-smeared appearance brought the warrior quickly to obedience.

"If you will climb aboard, sir, I think we can——" But Blade did not wait for the man to finish his invitation. He leaped down onto the deck of the galley and began pacing back and forth. The warriors jumped down after him and shouted orders to the rowers. Water foamed, oars squealed, and the galley backed free and swung around to join the pursuit of Piralu.

The galley swept through the Chiribuan line and raced north. The sails were kept tightly furled to reduce wind resistance. But the oars pounded steadily. Over their pounding came the sharper cracks of whips as the oarmasters laid on the lash. Occasional splashes told of buckets of river water dumped over the lash-scarred, sweating backs of the slaves at the oars.

Half an hour went by. The Chiribuan fleet was almost out of sight to the south, the galleys chasing Piralu well in sight to the north. And Blade could even make out the dark shape of Piralu's galley beyond the masts of his pursuers. He swore until he had no breath left for swearing or speech. The stroke that Piralu and the cult had launched had fallen short, but Piralu still lived. Blade wanted to change that.

In another half hour the fleet was gone and the galleys ahead visibly closer. But how long could the slaves below sustain the pace?

Blade turned to the warriors standing by the railing. "Warriors of Chiribu! We'll have to relieve the slaves at the oars if we want to catch up with the others in time." He started unbuckling his sword belt.

"But—" There were looks of blank amazement all around him.

"Do we want to let the other galleys cut us out of all share in avenging King Hurakun?" Now there were appalled looks all around Blade. "Then let's grab the oars and start pulling." He bent to throw open the hatch to the slave hold. His example, his manner, and his appearance swept away all resistance. He was in one of those moods that made it all but impossible to disobey him.

Now he could not tell how fast they were catching up, because his world was the dark smelly hold of the galley, the thunder of the oars, the murmur of water outside the planks. He poured his strength into his oar until he began to wonder if he would have any left to swing a sword or climb the side of Piralu's galley. But he did not miss a stroke in those brief moments of doubt.

After some vague time a shout came from on deck. "We're up with the squadron!" The still weary slaves were led back to their benches, and Blade led the warriors back on deck. The men aboard the other galleys now on either side of them stared in confusion at the grimy, sweat-dripping men emerging from the hold of Blade's galley to pick up their swords and axes.

They did not have much time to stare, though, and none to make any remarks. Suddenly Piralu's big galley swung sharply to the right, driving for the bank of the river. Blade's eyes turned toward the shore. Flickers of movement among the trees caught his eye; he saw a white bat-mask flashing in the sun.

"He's got men from the temples of Ayocan waiting ashore," Blade shouted, pointing. "We've got to cut him off, get in front of him."

The galley surged forward again as the oarmasters laid on their whips more frantically than ever. It took the lead. The gap of water between it and Piralu's galley began to narrow faster than the gap between Piralu's galley and the shore.

Blade shouted war cries and brandished his weapons as

he saw that. He was at the thin edge of reason now, with no thought for anything except the galley that loomed ahead—higher—higher—higher.

Then in one instant it seemed to tower above Blade like a mountain wall as it ran violently aground. In the next instant Blade's own galley ploughed in among the enemy's oars. Wood snapped and cracked. From the enemy's hold came the screams of galley slaves mangled by the flailing oar-handles. Blade's galley kept surging forward, splintering more oars, until its bow rammed hard against the side of Piralu's ship.

The shock as it did so nearly sent Blade hurtling clear into the river. But he caught himself with one hand and one foot, and pulled himself back aboard. An axe whistled down past his head and went *chunk* into the deck while he was doing so. He pulled it free, then looked up at the deck of Piralu's galley. His arm whipped up, the axe sparked in the sun as it flew through the air, then sparked again as it split a Holy Warrior's head open. Before the man had fallen to the deck, Blade was swarming up the side of the enemy ship.

Without a trace of the "tree of death's" drug in him, he was very nearly as mad as one of the Death-Vowed. His mask was blood—most of it other people's—rather than a bat's head. But his war cries were as blood-curdling, and his weapons struck with greater force and far greater skill. He was as terrifying as any three Death-Vowed ever launched into battle by the cult. When he burst over the railing of the galley, his arrival alone cleared a space in front of him. Death-Vowed and Holy Warriors and Piralu's household fighters alike scattered in all directions. Some of them lost their heads so thoroughly that they leaped clean over the side, and their screams increased the uproar.

Blade did not wait for any more warriors from his galley to join him, but charged straight into the enemy. Now he had Piralu almost in his grasp, and he was damned if he was going to let the Second Prince get away!

The men facing Blade now did not give way before his

charge, largely because they could not. He had to carve his way into their ranks with sword and axe. But few of the men he struck down struck back. The deck underfoot became slick with blood and littered with bodies. Foot by foot, Blade fought his way aft toward the cabin where Piralu's standard hung from the door. Behind him he could hear more shouts and the clash of more weapons as the warriors from the other galleys joined in the fight. From the sounds they were moving forward, pushing the enemy toward the bow.

Blade had just beaten a Holy Warrior to the deck with the flat of his sword when the cabin door burst open with a crash. Blade sprang back, raising sword and axe to meet Piralu's charge. But the figure that burst out into the daylight was not Piralu. It stood nearly seven feet high, its head was a white bat-mask set on a dark blue body, and great leathery wings swept back from its shoulders. Axes swung in both clawed hands. Screams of terror rose behind Blade, and the sounds of spreading panic.

Blade knew perfectly well that this was the Supreme Brother of the cult in his ceremonial garb. But he would have gone into the attack knowing that he faced the god himself. His sword blurred in the air as it whistled toward the man's head, then clanged off an axe that rose to meet it. Blade struck with his own axe, and again there was a crash of weapons meeting harmlessly in midair.

And again, and again. Blade doubted that the Supreme Brother would have been able to match him so well under normal circumstances. But the priest was coming to the battle fresh. Blade had already poured out buckets of sweat and a fair amount of blood.

After a dozen exchanges Blade knew that he was not going to be able to get through his opponent's guard. The Supreme Brother's mind seem to leap ahead, to discover Blade's moves almost before Blade's own mind had formed them. This realization touched off a moment of doubt in Blade's mind. But that passed, and its place was taken by memory. In this dimension no one seemed to know anything about unarmed combat.

Blade still felt no emotion, other than a sense of frustration that this fight with the priest was keeping him from reaching Piralu. He had been doing his best to keep the Supreme Brother with his back to the railing. Now he abandoned that, letting the priest take the initiative. Gradually the two men swung about on the blood-smeared deck, until Blade was backed almost against the railing.

Almost. He was careful to leave a space behind him, a space he measured in a quick glance. In the next glance, he saw that the Supreme Brother was going to try to drive him back, wipe out that space, push him over the railing. The timing of his own next move would have to be nearly perfect.

The Supreme Brother rocked back on his heels, then drove in at Blade. Blade pretended to slip, dropping down flat on his back on the boards, his head just clearing the railing. The Supreme Brother gave a shrill yell of triumph, and raised both axes high, leaning forward to strike down at Blade's head and chest. The axes began their descent.

In that moment Blade's feet shot up like a piston. They shot into the priest's stomach, scooping him up into the air, up, up, over Blade's head as Blade rolled back on his shoulders—up, and clear over the railing. Blade's head crashed into something solid. For a moment the world swirled around him. But the sounds he heard—or did not hear—told him what he wanted to know.

The Supreme Priest had no time to change his scream of triumph into one of terror before he struck the water. He did scream as he splashed into the river, and once more after that. Blade heard nothing more, because the splashings of the little fish were not loud enough to rise above the sounds of battle. Blood was pouring from his throbbing head as he staggered to his feet. He was in time to see the last of the air burble out of the Supreme Brother's batmask, and see it sink out of sight—dragged down by the weight of the now fleshless skull inside it.

Blade leaned over the railing, conscious that his last reserves of strength were gone, and that his head was throbbing agonizingly. He managed to pull himself straight and turn forward, toward the remainder of the battle.

As he did so, the pain in his head suddenly flared and spread until from crown to chin his head was one raw, tearing agony. The world dissolved. But he could still feel the deck under his feet, know that he was lurching toward the railing, up against it—and over it.

His mouth opened in a scream that died in a gurgle as he struck the water and the river poured into his mouth. He was in the river, bleeding, down among the deadly fish. The computer had him, but it might let him go, and then the fish would eat him and there would be no brain of his left for the computer to—

The computer did not let go. Blade felt a stab of pain in his leg as one of the fish took a bite. Then the pain in his head swelled further, the world's redness pulsed and quivered, then it was no longer red but black. And after that it was no longer anything.

CHAPTER 21

There was a faint *click* in the silent library as Lord Leighton switched the tape recorder off. The silence returned, more thickly than ever. Outside J's flat a drizzling rain was falling, but the thick curtains over the windows kept both sound and the street lights out.

J let out his breath in a long whistling sigh. "No wonder Blade was in such a foul temper when he came back. Doesn't get to take a crack at the fellow responsible for all that rumpus on the river, doesn't get to bring back a sample of the healing drug, and nearly gets eaten alive by the river fish before we can bring him home. He must have ended up feeling that all fates were against him."

Leighton nodded, but it was obvious to J that the scientist's mind was somewhere else. Finally he stood up and began pacing around the room, hands clasped behind his back and head bowed.

"J, we've absolutely got to push for a breakthrough on the Controlled Return Project. We've got to be able to send Blade—"

"Or somebody," put in J.

"Or somebody," said Leighton, testy at the interruption. "But we've got to be able to get back to this dimension and find those plants. Even a sample might be enough. If we could get even one of those pads, we could turn it over to the chemists and get it analyzed. And then turn the analysis over to one of the pharmaceutical firms, and we'd be able to give England a complete dominance of the pharmaceutical market."

181

"Not to mention all the lives that would be saved," said J quietly.

"To be sure, to be sure," said Leighton. "But you do agree with me, don't you, J? We've simply got to get somebody back to this dimension. It's as important in a way as the dimension of the Menel."

Considerably more important, thought J. The discovery of the nonhuman Menel in the Dimension of the Ice Dragons was earth-shaking enough, but rather remote from the average man's concerns. But the discovery of the healing drug that the cult of Ayocan extracted from the bush by the lake was something that would instantly justify the Project in the eyes of the most conservative and hard-headed M.P. or his constituents. And there were always the lives that could be saved. How many thousands or tens of thousands each year? J didn't know. He didn't even feel qualified to guess. But he had to admit he liked the idea of giving England something that would help heal, not kill, from the Project. He had dealt with death and secrets of death for most of his life. He would like a change.

And he would also like a change for Blade. The chap was certain to be willing to go back, but damn it, there was such a thing as flogging a willing horse! And if the Controlled Return technique was ever perfected, it would almost certainly mean that Blade would go on making trips into Dimension X. Even if they found a new man for trips into new dimensions, they would still need Blade to go back into the old ones, the ones that he had pioneered. Would perfecting Controlled Return amount in fact to a death sentence for Blade?

Perhaps. But J knew that he could not stand in the way of what England needed—what the world needed. And certainly not anything like this healing drug. He could not and would not, because Blade himself would not want him to.

"All right," J said. "Shall I arrange an appointment with the Prime Minister?"

"Yes," said Leighton. "Do that."

ALL NEW DYNAMITE SERIES

THE DESTROYER

by Richard Sapir & Warren Murphy

CURE, the world's most secret crime-fighting organization created the perfect weapon — Remo Williams — man programmed to become a cold, calculating death machine. The super man of the 70's!

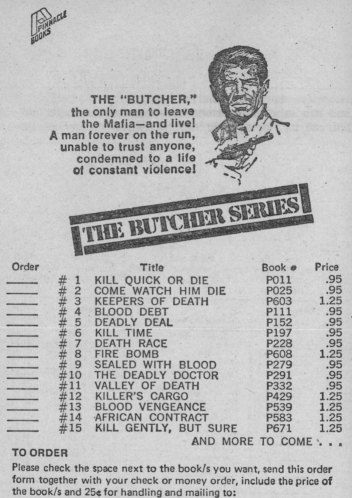